THE WISH

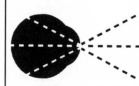

This Large Print Book carries the
Seal of Approval of N.A.V.H.

VIRGINIA WEDDINGS, BOOK 3

THE WISH

A ROMANCE PERSEVERES IN THE COMMONWEALTH

LAURALEE BLISS

THORNDIKE PRESS

A part of Gale, Cengage Learning

GALE
CENGAGE Learning™

Detroit • New York • San Francisco • New Haven, Conn • Waterville, Maine • London

LIBRARY OF CONGRESS CATALOGING-IN-PUBLICATION DATA

Bliss, Lauralee.
    The wish : a romance perseveres in the commonwealth / by
Lauralee Bliss.
        p. cm. — (Virginia weddings ; bk. 3) (Thorndike Press large
    print Christian romance)
        ISBN-13: 978-1-4104-0618-7 (hardcover : alk. paper)
        ISBN-10: 1-4104-0618-0 (hardcover : alk. paper)
        1. Virginia — Fiction. 2. Large type books. I. Title.
    PS3602.L575W57 2008
    813'.6—dc22   2008001124

Published in 2008 by arrangement with Barbour Publishing, Inc.

Printed in the United States of America
1 2 3 4 5 6 7 12 11 10 09 08

DEDICATION

To Kathy Icenhour,
an encourager and prayer partner in times
of need.
This smile's for you!
This book is written in fond memory of
the beautiful residents I cared for as a
nurse's aide at the Ulster County
Infirmary, Kingston, New York, in the
1980s.
They taught me a great deal — how to
laugh, to love, and what it means to care
for one another.

Dear Reader,

What a beautiful area to kindle a romance — in sight of Virginia's mysterious yet awesome Blue Ridge Mountains. In *Virginia Weddings,* you are about to undertake a journey of the heart, soul, and spirit as couples, both young and old, solve mysteries while finding romance.

Just as I experienced love here on a mountain summit in Virginia some nineteen years ago, I welcome you to join these heroines and heroes who overcome their difficulties to discover enduring love within the realm of breathtaking and rejuvenating scenery. I hope their stories of faith will touch your life and fill you with the knowledge of God's unending love and concern for you.

I welcome you to visit my Web site at www .lauraleebliss.com to discover other books that will uplift your spirit while providing page-turning entertainment.

May God bless you.

Lauralee

CHAPTER 1

"Ouch, that hurt!"

Debbie Reilly yanked her finger away to observe the trickle of blood oozing out. She climbed down the stepladder and dodged the string of Christmas lights that dangled from the doorway into the third-floor nurses' lounge.

"What happened?" inquired the registered nurse, Mrs. Whitaker. She stood by her cart of medications, pouring pills into cups to distribute during the coming noon hour.

"Must be a broken bulb up there or something." Debbie strode off to the clean utility room to find a bandage. From the hallway of the White Pines Health Care Facility where she worked as a nursing assistant, Debbie could hear the variety of voices emanating from the rooms of the residents. There were Harold White, a World War II veteran who complained about the rations he had to eat; Sylvia Hubble, who babbled about working in a dress shop; and Delores Masterson, who stroked and talked to a pretend cat nestled in her lap. A few others were calling out the names of loved ones.

Debbie fetched a bandage from a box. She began removing the wrapper when, above the noises in the hall, she heard a faint voice like that of an angel, singing a song from days gone by. Debbie smiled to herself as she neatly wrapped the bandage around her sliced finger. The singing beckoned her to the room, and Debbie peeked in to find Elvina Jenson struggling to force her chubby arm through the sleeve of a blouse.

"Let me help you with that," Debbie said to her.

A smile spread across her plump face. "Thank you so much, dear."

Debbie helped her fit one arm at a time through the sleeves, then buttoned the blouse down the front. She stepped back and watched the unseeing gray blue eyes of the woman stare straight ahead from where she sat on the edge of the hospital bed.

"Now, would you mind getting me my earrings?" Elvina asked.

Debbie opened the drawer of the nightstand to fish out the pair of gold earrings Elvina insisted on wearing every day. When she did, her leg brushed a rectangular box sitting on a stool. Debbie handed Elvina the earrings, then turned to see the gift tag still attached to the top with a piece of tape. Bits of Christmas wrapping paper clung to the sides of the leather case. *To Gram,* she read on the tag, *With love always, Nathaniel J.* "An early Christmas gift?" she inquired of Elvina whose fingers fumbled to attach the pretty gold earrings to her earlobes. "Or a late Thanksgiving gift?"

Her head turned in the direction of Debbie's voice. "What was that?"

"The box here. I hadn't noticed it before, but I see the tag on it."

Elvina's face again broke open into a broad smile. "Oh, my box. Nathaniel gave it to me last evening. He said he couldn't wait but insisted that I have it now. We laughed at the songs we played on it last night. I love it so much."

Debbie furrowed her forehead in puzzlement. "You mean it plays music?"

"Of course, dear. It's a record player."

Debbie unfastened the twin clasps and lifted the lid to find an old-fashioned turntable, arm, and needle that fit into the grooves of the record. "You don't see these around," she confessed. "I remember my family owning one when I was little. Then, one day, they became obsolete. Now we have Internet downloads. A whole new wave of music."

"Nathaniel is so kind," the older lady continued. "He told me about those fancy music boxes they have nowadays, but I wanted my record player. You see, mine was taken from the house when I came here. Most of my most precious things were sold." Debbie watched the tears well up in the woman's eyes. "But Nathaniel searched in antique shops all over the Roanoke area until he found one exactly like my old one. He wouldn't tell me what he paid for it. Can you imagine?" She shook her head. "And to think that things like that would end up in an antique store. Now, can you help me put on my lipstick?"

Debbie went once more to the drawer, sifting through the combs, bobby pins, and other assorted junk tucked inside before finding the tube of lipstick. Elvina sat patiently on the bed while Debbie traced Elvina's dry lips with color. In an afterthought, she put a dab of lipstick on each pale cheek and rubbed it in lightly to produce a blush.

Elvina chuckled. "Trying to doll me up so I can get a man?"

Debbie's cheeks heated at Elvina's question. "Why not? You're young at heart."

Elvina laughed merrily. "You're so sweet. I was hoping you would be working today. I tell Nathaniel all the time about my nurse who comes and takes care of me during the day. He's still single, you know. I tell him all the time he needs to settle down. But he has his own way of doing things." She reached out and patted Debbie's arm. "Do you have a man in your life?"

Debbie slid the cover over the tube of lipstick and tossed it back into the drawer. "No man yet." She tried to suppress the thought that stirred up a wave of emotion.

"That's too bad. How old are you, dear?"

"Twenty-eight."

"Dear me. Twenty-eight and no man. I had four babies by the time I was your age. I had six children, you know."

Debbie gazed at the picture frame decorating the bedside table. In the middle of the portrait sat Elvina in a huge chair, surrounded by her family. Two men and three women stood beside the chair, all with graying hair. A host of grandchildren and great-grandchildren formed a semicircle around them. The photographer probably had to use a hefty, wide-angle lens to capture all the smiling faces that comprised the huge family. For a moment, Debbie wondered which one in the photograph was this Nathaniel whom Elvina so highly praised.

As if Elvina could see Debbie examining the photo, she said, "Six babies, even though there are only five in the picture. One was killed in Vietnam. Albert, my oldest. He was Nathaniel's father."

Debbie focused once more on the old record player and the writing scrawled on a gift tag in the shape of a Christmas bell. *Nathaniel J.* "The *J* must stand for his middle name?" she wondered out loud.

"Nathaniel James," Elvina supplied. "He signs everything to me *Nathaniel J.* He's just like his father, with his own way of doing things. I so wish Nathaniel could have known his father, but Nathaniel wasn't even born when Albert died in a helicopter crash over Vietnam. Albert was just like his father before him, you see, joining the army and all."

Debbie listened while Elvina reminisced about her family. She wished she could stay all day and listen to her stories. The time displayed on a small alarm clock alerted her to the work she still needed to accomplish before noon, including hanging the rest of the colored lights over the doorway of the nurses' lounge. "Let me help you into your wheelchair, Elvina," she said as she slid a pair of shoes on over the cotton socks Elvina wore to bed every night. "Then I have to run and check on a few of the other residents." Elvina nodded and held up her arms. Debbie bent her knees, encircled the resident with her arms, and slowly propelled her into a wheelchair outfitted with a soft pad. She placed a flowered robe across Elvina's lap, then took up a comb and gently fluffed out her curly gray hair.

"You always do such a nice job," Elvina commented. "Now before you leave, would you mind putting on a record for me?"

Debbie turned to the box, unfastened the clasps once more, and lifted the top. Beside the box lay several records. "You want to hear the one about the doggy in the window?"

"That would be fine. It's my favorite."

Debbie slipped the record out of its jacket, placed the large disc on the turntable, and positioned the needle carefully on the record. A scratching noise came through the small speakers inside the box before the female vocalist began the opening bars of Elvina's favorite song. The tune followed Debbie out into the corridor, where several of the residents in their wheelchairs had paused in the hallway to listen. She returned to the string of lights still hanging from the doorway, examining the bulbs, one by one, for the culprit that had lacerated her finger.

"What's that racket I hear?" asked Trish. The fellow nursing assistant sat inside the lounge sipping a mug of coffee.

"Elvina's record player." Debbie yanked out the broken bulb. "Do we have any extra bulbs?"

"Look in the first drawer on the left at the nurses' station," Trish replied. "You know, I haven't heard a song like that since I visited Granny's house when I was little. 'Course that was before my parents split up. Never got to see her after that. Then she died."

Debbie pulled out the drawer to fetch a package of bulbs. "Elvina's grandson bought the record player for her. He found one like her original in an antique store."

"So that's what the mystery gift was," said Trish. Debbie couldn't help but peer inside the lounge at the aide who sat there smirking. "Her grandson came strutting in here last week while I worked an evening shift, saying he was buying his grandma a gift to remember. Wish he would get me a gift to remember . . . like a diamond ring."

"A diamond ring!" Debbie said in astonishment, mounting the stepladder to finish fastening the string of lights above the doorway.

16

"You've never met the hunky grandson? Wow, is all I can say. And he's so devoted to her. What guy do you know comes in almost every evening to spend time with an old lady? Guess that's why he's not married. No social life. Though he can come here anytime his little ol' heart desires, just as long as he eventually asks me out. Better yet, make it a marriage proposal. I'm not getting any younger."

Debbie fumbled with the tacks, trying to stick them into the wall above the doorway to anchor the lights, but she found Trish's words distracting.

"Normally I never pay attention to the visitors who come walking in here," Trish went on. "You can't help but notice him, though. Tall. Huge shoulders. Wavy dark hair and eyes to die for. I'll bet he's the reason everyone on the evening shift wants to be assigned to the rooms in the front hall. They fight like cats and dogs over who will take care of Elvina so they can spend time with the handsome grandson."

Debbie could just imagine the nurses on the evening shift, circling the nurse in charge like a pack of wolves and fighting over the string of rooms located in the front corridor. She never once considered asking for certain rooms just so she could interact with the visitors. For some reason, Mrs. Whitaker always assigned her room 307 where Elvina resided. It became routine. But now with all this talk of the handsome grandson, Debbie wondered if she should switch to the evening shift for a week, just to see what the hubbub was about. Then she thought better of it. Trish and the gang would no doubt vie for the treasured room. As it was, Debbie couldn't stand how Trish cared for the residents. Trish took shortcuts that irritated her to no end.

"All done," Debbie announced, stepping back to admire the colored lights glimmering from the doorway. Around the nursing station, she had strung a rope of plastic holly and berries. Inside the lounge, a Christmas tree decorated a far table that once held the huge coffeepot. Another tree of red ribbons and white lights decorated the inside of the solarium where the residents congregated for meals, entertainment, or television. Debbie always found the holidays difficult at the facility. Some of the residents would become depressed at the idea of spending the most celebrated time of the year cooped up inside a health-care facility rather than at home with relatives. A few were fortunate enough to have families willing to keep them over the holidays, but most spent their holidays here with the nursing staff. Knowing she was scheduled to work on Christmas, Debbie was determined to make the time as festive as possible. She made a mental list of the things she wanted to do — bake up a batch of Christmas cookies for those who could have sweets, coax the church youth choir into performing a selection of Christmas carols at the facility on Christmas Eve, and buy a few gifts for her favorite residents, like Elvina. For a moment, she wondered what this Nathaniel would think if she came walking in on Christmas morning with a gift for his grandma — like a few new records to play on the ancient record player. Would he smile at her and show her some interest?

Forget it, Debbie. Don't get yourself all worked up. You've managed to strike out with every guy you've ever met. Remember how the one you loved ended up marrying your roommate? So don't set yourself up for further disappointment. Debbie sighed, recalling with pain her close friendship with Brad. She always assumed one day their friendship would turn to love — until she discovered his real interest lay with her roommate, Tonya. When the fact came to light, Debbie felt both betrayed and used. Brad and Tonya were now married and living in Washington,

D.C., with their two kids. She received a Christmas picture card from them every year, and every year, she would gaze at his handsome face and think of all she had lost. *Guess I'm just not cut out for love.*

Despite this, the thought of Nathaniel, whoever he might be, sent a snippet of hope rising up within her. Perhaps some day he would discover that it was she who kept his grandma looking so fine each day. Maybe then he would want to find out more about her. *Dream on. He won't even notice me among all the rest here. I'm one out of many.*

Debbie strolled over to her small steel cart to put away the linens left from the morning care, still thinking about the man called Nathaniel J. He must be a one-of-a-kind guy to forgo a social life to spend evenings with Elvina. Even going to great lengths to find her a treasured keepsake like the record player. Debbie inhaled a breath. *I would like to meet him someday, even if it goes no further than that.*

Debbie stepped out into the frigid December air after a long day at work. Inhaling the breath of wind that brushed her face, she detected the faint scent of smoke drifting from a nearby fireplace or woodstove. Her feet scuffed along the slick sidewalk, still covered by patches of ice from a recent storm. The cold wind ripped through her jacket while she gazed up into the darkening skies above. Behind her stood the brick building of the White Pines Health Care Facility, framed by a grove of pine trees, glazed with ice, which gave the facility its name. Twin wreaths decorated the front doors. White lights glimmered in pretty array on the bushes. A few cars drifted into the parking lot, bearing visitors who came to sit with their loved ones through the dinner hour. She watched them arrive one by one, wondering which one might be this Nathaniel J. Some were older people dressed in their heavy wool coats. Others toted children along with them. Debbie smiled, knowing how much the elderly residents loved seeing the faces of children. Every year, Debbie coordinated a Christmas Eve performance and a few youth groups would come to the facility to sing traditional Christmas carols, including the youth group from her own church. At that moment, she wished the group could sing Elvina's favorite song about the doggy in the window. Debbie smiled, thinking how surprised Elvina would be if the group suddenly broke out into the song from long ago. She could imagine the scene — the tears drifting slowly down Elvina's plump cheeks, her gnarled hand fumbling to find Debbie's and give a squeeze of gratitude. "You made my day," her voice would crack. And standing behind her, smiling in approval, would be her grandson, Nathaniel J.

Stop it, Debbie, she scolded herself. *Get the guy out of your head. He's probably already got a girlfriend, for all you know.*

She continued down the road, still thinking about an encounter with Elvina's grandson, when her feet flew out from underneath her. She fell hard on her backside in the road, just as a car swerved around the bend to enter the parking lot of the facility. Brakes squealed as the car came to an abrupt halt by the curb opposite her. Debbie slowly sat up, her tailbone screaming in pain.

"Are you all right?" inquired an anxious voice.

"Yeah," she sputtered, trying to get to her feet. Instead, she felt a shooting pain running down each leg. Her legs wobbled, and she collapsed onto the road with a grunt.

"Here, let me give you a hand." A tall figure, dressed in a wool overcoat, offered her his gloved hand. She grasped his hand, squeezing her eyes shut to ward off the pain, and gingerly got to her feet.

"It's pretty slippery out here," said the

man's voice.

"Yeah," Debbie mumbled again, hobbling along the sidewalk. "Thanks."

"Can you drive?"

"My car's in the garage. I walked today. My apartment's not that far. I can make it."

"Pretty dangerous to be walking in this kind of weather along a major highway. I'll gladly give you a lift."

Debbie stared into his dark eyes, and he peered back in concern. He didn't seem to fit the description of someone trying to take advantage of her. No doubt he was a visitor coming to see someone at the facility. "I'm fine, but thanks for the offer." Debbie continued down the road, even as her back erupted into spasms with every step she took. Once more her feet slipped on the ice. She would have fallen a second time had she not, at the last moment, grabbed hold of a young tree at the corner.

"I don't think you're going to make it without doing more harm than good," the man said, rushing to her side. He offered her his arm.

"You don't need to help me. I'm sure you've got things to do. I'm okay, really."

"You're not okay. If you're as close as you say, it probably won't take me ten minutes, tops, to drive you home. I have plenty of time. I'm meeting a fine lady, and she won't mind if I'm being a hero in disguise. She likes heroes."

So he has a girlfriend who works at the facility, Debbie thought. *Guess there's no harm in getting a lift then.* She allowed him to guide her to his car. She eased herself into the passenger seat, wincing in pain as the tender area of her back pressed against the seat.

"I take it you work at White Pines," he said, pointing at her baby blue nursing pants that peeked out from beneath the coat she wore and her white clogs in desperate need of polish.

"I just got off the day shift. Normally I get off at three, but they needed a few extra hands for a couple of hours until help arrived. It looks like I may be working late the rest of this week."

"How long have you worked at White Pines?"

"Eight years," Debbie said. She hunkered down in the seat and watched the scenery flash by. "When you get to town, turn right at the next stop sign. My apartment building is on the left."

"Do you like nursing?"

"It's okay. The holidays are tough, though. We try to do what we can to make it special

24

for the residents."

He steered the car into an empty space in front of the building.

"Thanks a lot."

"Sure. You need help getting to the door?" He added quickly, "Of course I won't go in or anything. I just want to make sure you don't fall."

Debbie detected a gentlemanly quality about him that put to rest any remaining fears. She accepted his assistance and grasped the crook of his proffered elbow.

He paused at the door. "Better put some ice on that bump you have and take some ibuprofen." He laughed. "Hey, wait a minute. Why should I be telling you what to do? You're a nurse."

"A nursing assistant," she corrected.

"What's the difference?"

"I didn't earn a college degree. LPNs and RNs have degrees and a license to practice. I took a training course, but that's all. I don't deal with medications, procedures, that sort of thing. I basically take care of the residents' needs like bathing, dressing, feeding, etc."

He nodded his head. "I see. You do all the labor."

"I guess so, in a way. Though the RNs have to make all the tough decisions. I've thought of one day getting a full-fledged degree, but I'm not sure I could take the stress of being the boss." Her smile ignited a grin on his face. His bright teeth matched the bit of snow that frosted the bushes. "You'd better get going so you aren't late for your date."

His dark eyebrows lifted at the comment before another grin swept across his face. "My date," he repeated. "I'll have to tell her that one. She'd get a kick out of it. Take care of yourself, and no more spills. Ice can hurt." He nodded and strode to his car.

Debbie watched his departure from her doorway as he turned the car around in the parking area and sped off in the direction of White Pines. She leaned against the door frame before the shooting pain in her back reminded her of her need for rest. *So long, my wonderful benefactor,* she thought with a sigh. *Too bad you already have someone else.*

CHAPTER 2

"Hey, Gram."

"Nathaniel, I just knew it was you walking through the door. I can tell because you're wearing that Blue Ice cologne I gave you." Her face erupted into a broad smile. "Now you sit right here by me and tell me how your day went."

"You never change," he said with a smile, stooping to kiss her wrinkled cheek. He withdrew at that moment to find a small blotch of color on her cheeks. "Where did the blush come from? I don't remember Aunt Grace sending any blush. Just tubes of that hot red lipstick."

"It's my little nurse who takes care of me during the day, don't you know? She put some on my face. I told her I'm all set now to meet a man."

He snickered as he sat down beside her and took her hand in his. "Gram, you're something else."

"I asked her if she had a man, and she said no. Maybe you should see if she's right for you?"

Neil, as he was nicknamed by his friends and family, could only shake his head, even though Gram could not see the look on his face. She never changed but kept after him about the relationship thing as though it were a secret mission of hers. Just then a nurse from the evening shift bopped in for a moment and offered him her brightest smile. Soon after, she came strolling in again with a tray bearing cups of ice, sodas, and Gram's favorite sugar cookies, freshly baked in the facility kitchen. *Not again,* he groaned to himself. He began feeling more and more uncomfortable visiting Gram in the evening with all the nurses who came snooping around the room. Some, like this one, offered goodies. Others asked him questions about work, interests, cars, and the like. He knew they were trying to determine his eligibility. Gram always laughed at the attention and poked him in the arm, asking him when he would invite one of the young ladies out.

"Nurses aren't my type," he would tell her.

"Why not? They're caring individuals."

Neil twisted his lips. *Not this crew. They are looking to make a conquest, like I'm the*

Bachelor of the Year or something.

"Nathaniel, you're upset," Gram now said. "I can tell by the way you're holding my hand. Is it the evening nurse who just came in?"

"She's doing the usual routine to make some kind of impression. Your cookies, my soda. I'm surprised she didn't give me a business card with her phone number on it and the nights she's available for dinner."

"Oh, you," Gram said, squeezing his hand. "None of them can help it. You're a wonderful young man. This wouldn't be happening if you found yourself the right girl to settle down with."

"She's nowhere around here, I can tell you that."

"What about Roanoke? It's a very large city with plenty of fine ladies. Maybe a coworker at that insurance place where you work? Or your church?"

How could he tell his grandmother that out of all the coworkers in the place, one was already married, one was divorced with three kids, and another was old enough to be his mother? In church, the women were either fresh out of college and just beginning to taste life or already married. No one in the middle, like him. The lonely middle man.

"The trouble with you is that you don't go out enough. You spend too many evenings here instead of going to where the young people are. I used to love attending the opera with Joe, you know. Why don't you do something like that?"

Neil nearly laughed at the suggestion but kept his lips pressed tight. Still, he could envision himself decked out in a tuxedo with a lovely lady in evening apparel on his arm. Perhaps the suggestion wouldn't be so farfetched if there were a lovely woman to escort to such a venue. He'd had a few female interests in the past, but nothing came of them. Between work and then coming here for nightly visits, as Gram said, there wasn't much time.

"Gram, I don't go out because I would miss seeing you. You're my lady friend. In fact, the nurse I helped out today thought I was going on a date."

Elvina straightened in her wheelchair. "You helped a nurse? When? Where?"

"She took a fall on the ice and landed right in the road. She refused my help at first, but I talked her into letting me drive her home."

"Do you like her? Since you come here every day, you could see her at the same time. Something like that would work."

"Gram, let it go."

"I would, except for the fact you're the son of my oldest boy. Not to mention that you're thirty-five years old. That's too old. I want you to find a wife and have children. I want another Nathaniel in the family."

He laughed. "I'd think having one around is enough for you."

"It's never enough." She sighed. "Oh, if only you'd known your father. You're so much like him. He married your mother late, too. He gave me the same excuses. There was no one he liked. He was too busy to care, anyway. So I guess I should expect his son to do the same."

Neil said little. There wasn't much to say. Whenever anyone talked about his father, he listened politely.

"And the little nurse who takes care of me during the day is twenty-eight years old. Can you imagine? Twenty-eight and never been married. Tsk, tsk."

"People are waiting longer to get married these days, Gram. They don't do it fresh out of high school like in the old days. They have careers, and they want to make sure that the one they're marrying is the right one. I prefer the idea of going slow. Maybe we wouldn't have so many divorces nowadays if people chose their mates better."

"If you go any slower, I won't live to attend your wedding, let alone enjoy any great-grandchildren. I want the son of my Albert to be happy."

He had heard how close his father and Gram were until his father ended up in the service and then died in Vietnam. For years after, Gram had struggled with depression, only cheering up whenever his mother brought him and his siblings over for a visit. Now as an adult, Neil's visits with his grandmother continued as they had back then. He felt a special bond with Gram because of it all. Over the years, she had shared all she could remember about his father, to the point that Neil felt he knew him, even if he'd never met him. And it probably cheered Gram to know that, though he was the product of a son who lived no more, something of his father, Albert, still lived on. It would have been great, of course, to have a dad. Someone to take him to baseball games. Someone to lean on when the going got rough. Even someone to talk to about these women issues. But he let it go as he did with most things. God had His reasons, even if Neil didn't understand them all.

After dinner, Neil bade Gram farewell and headed for the elevator. Passing by the nursing station, he ignored the stares from every corner and the faces peeking out from the lounge. Heat flooded his cheeks. If only he could come here for a visit without thinking he was a chunk of meat on display. As it was, he never considered himself the type with that kind of appeal. In the mirror, he saw a normal guy with brown hair and eyes to match. There were no dimples, no flashy smile, nothing that should attract this amount of attention. Maybe there were no other guys his age visiting the residents. And for certain, the ratio of single men to women in this small town left much to be desired.

For now, he decided to dismiss the thought of women and think about Gram and what he would like to give her for Christmas. He had an idea brewing and wondered if he could make it work. What if he could arrange to have her taken out of this facility to spend Christmas with his mother and siblings? Christmas at home, surrounded by her loved ones, would be the ultimate present, in his opinion — a wish come true for Gram, and one she would treasure always. He would take her to his home if he could, but a high-rise apartment in downtown Roanoke was hardly the place for a wheelchair-bound woman. His mother had plenty of room, if he could convince her. He would make it as easy as possible. Arrange for everything and hire a nurse to help.

He strode out into the cold night for the drive home to Roanoke. All around were the signs of the blossoming holiday season — twinkle lights glimmering from homes, shop windows bursting with unusual gift ideas, bell ringers for charity organizations stationed in front of the shopping centers, and even the faint hum of a distant carol in the air. He thought about presents and the great idea of bringing Gram home for the holidays. He could just imagine her face on the big day when he rolled her into the family home to greet her loved ones. He had to make it happen somehow.

Suddenly the injured nurse on the road came to the forefront of his thoughts. He could chat with her about the idea and what equipment he might need. Maybe he could even hire her. She seemed to care about the residents. She had experience, working there at White Pines for eight years. Maybe she would do it if the price was right. The thought buzzed in his head as he drove along, making a mental note to arrive at the same time tomorrow in the hopes of catching the nurse on her way home.

■ ■ ■ ■

Another busy workday at the White Pines facility had come and gone when Debbie emerged from the building, bleary-eyed from the lack of sleep over her bruised tailbone and worn-out from having to float to another floor because of a nursing shortage. She still shuddered over the day's work — contending with several belligerent residents who, as they put it, "did not like her style of nursing." She missed the peace of her own unit and the residents she had come to know and love. Now she looked forward to a relaxing bath, then curling up in front of the fireplace with a good book — if she could get a fire going in the small fireplace inside her apartment. Camping and fire building were not her forte. In Girl Scouts, she specialized in selling those great cookies. That and earning the first aid badge. She loved bandaging and caring for the sick.

Debbie took the walk slow this time, careful to avoid the glistening ice that gave her the colorful mark decorating her backside. She was so intent on staring at the pavement she did not hear a car pull up beside her until a voice startled her.

"Hello? Anybody home?"

Debbie whirled around to find a shadowy face peering at her from the car window. Shuddering, she ignored the car and continued on down the sidewalk. The car followed slowly behind. She began feeling hot in her jacket. Her nerves stood on edge, thinking of muggers who sometimes stalked young nurses walking home from work. If only she had her car back. She would be safe and sound, driving away at breakneck speed. *How long does it take for a garage to get the right parts anyway?*

"Is something the matter?" the voice persisted.

A car door slammed, followed by footsteps. Debbie searched for a place to run when she found herself face-to-face with a familiar figure dressed in a black overcoat.

"I didn't mean to scare you. I'm the guy who helped you out yesterday, remember?"

"Oh, it's you." She sighed in relief. "I'm not used to having strange men following me."

"Is your back doing better?"

Debbie shrugged. "I'll survive. It was hard today, trying to work with it. I never knew a bruised tailbone could hurt so much."

"Maybe you should take off a day or two and let it heal up."

"Call in sick this time of year? You must

36

be joking. As it is, everyone seems to be taking off early, leaving us very short-staffed. In fact, I had to work on another floor today, which was no fun. Different residents and different nursing personnel with their own philosophies and ways of doing things." She bent her head, studying the patches of ice decorating the sidewalk. "Then I had several residents who were not very friendly. One even swung his fist at me."

The man's eyes widened in alarm. He took a step closer. "Swung his fist at you? You're kidding."

"Don't worry. He missed. A good thing, too, or I'd have a bruise on my face to match the one on my tailbone."

"Look, it must still be hard walking, especially after a day like today. I can drive you home again. It's no trouble."

"What are you, the White Pines taxicab service?"

"When someone is injured and has had a rough day, I am. Better yet, how about we get ourselves some hot chocolate at the coffee shop in Daleville? I hear when life gives you lemons, drink chocolate."

She laughed. "You mean, when life gives you lemons, make lemonade."

"Hot chocolate in the winter. Lemonade in the summer."

Debbie snuggled her hands into the pockets of her jacket, feeling the warmth radiating through her at this friendly invite. Her first gift of chocolate, be it hot chocolate, presented by a good-looking man. Now that was a treat she could hardly turn down. "Sure, why not? I guess I deserve it."

He smiled and led the way back to his car. "By the way, I suppose we should introduce ourselves. I'm Neil."

"I'm Debbie."

He performed a U-turn and drove off in the direction of Daleville.

"So where do you work?" Debbie wondered. "Around here somewhere?"

"I live and work in Roanoke. I man a desk job at an insurance firm. Definitely not the fast lane."

"So you pick the pockets of the injured," she said with a laugh. "No wonder you were curious about my accident."

"I would be if your car was insured through my company and involved in an accident. I work in the auto division."

"Hey, maybe you can help me out. I've had my car in the garage now for five days. It seems they've lost the parts. Either that or they have the parts and don't know what to do with them. They were supposed to have my car fixed in a day or two. Something about replacing a few noisy valves. Now it's turning into a weeklong ordeal."

"Sounds fishy to me. If you want, I can stop by the garage and check it out for you."

Debbie sighed. A man of chocolate and a rescuer of one in the throes of being ripped off. She was more impressed by the minute. "That would be great. Thanks. It's Hank's Auto Service. I wonder if Hank knows what's going on. Anyway, I'd hate to think the garage is taking advantage of me just because I'm a woman. You never know." She gazed at the storefronts and homes, decked out in holiday greenery and lights. "Nary a Nativity scene to be found," she murmured.

"What was that?"

"Oh, I was just looking at all the worldly portrayals of the Christmas season. You know, elves, Santa, animals, stockings. But hardly any Nativity scenes and certainly none in the town squares. Too bad." She paused then, uncertain how he would take her opinions or the fact that she was a Christian.

"We live in strange times. No one has a need for God and especially no reminders of Him. Every major holiday is replaced by some symbol, like Easter bunnies for the Resurrection. And even the public schools call it winter break and not Christmas break

39

so one doesn't have to say the word *Christ*. It's crazy."

Debbie couldn't help but be delighted by his words, despite the seriousness of them. Neil thought the same way she did. This picture was getting rosier by the minute.

Sitting at the coffee shop a short time later, with a mug of hot chocolate topped off by a swirl of whipped cream, Debbie thought she had died and gone to heaven. She felt more relaxed than if she had submerged herself in that bathtub full of bubbles. Neil's dark eyes perusing her from across the table added to the pleasure. If not for the thought in the back of her mind about the date he had with a worker at White Pines yesterday, she might actually wonder if God was performing a wondrous miracle in her midst.

They talked about their days in school, their jobs, and what was on their wish list for Christmas. Debbie talked of owning a luxury SUV and laughed.

Neil shifted in his seat after draining his mug of chocolate and folded his hands on the table. "Debbie, there is another reason behind this little get-together."

Here it comes. He left the other nurse he's seeing at White Pines and wants to go out with me. She tried to hold her eagerness at bay, along with a twinge of anxiety. What if he did ask her out on a real date? What would she do? What would she wear? First things first. "Yes?"

"Since it's Christmas and we're talking about gifts, I have an extra special gift I'd like to give someone close to me. You see, I have a grandmother in White Pines who would love the best present of all — Christmas at home, surrounded by her family."

"So you visit your grandmother?"

"I go see her most evenings. That's where I was going when I saw you out there in the middle of the road."

Wow. So the date I thought he had with another woman in the facility was really a visit with his grandmother. What a guy. Kind, considerate, thoughtful of those in need. And looking pretty good right now. "That's sweet of you to think of her. Half the residents would love to go home to be with their families, but it just doesn't happen."

"I'm hoping I can make it happen for Gram. For as long as I can remember, she and I have always been close. Unusually so, I think, due to my father's death."

"I'm sorry to hear that."

"Don't be. I never knew him. My mother was carrying me at the time, so I never laid eyes on him. Anyway, I want to bring Gram

41

home to be with the family over the holidays. I have no space for her at my old bachelor pad in a high-rise. I need to convince Mom to go along with the idea, and I think hiring a nurse to take care of her might be just the ticket. I think Mom would agree to the plan, knowing I've already set up round-the-clock care. I would pay you well and —"

Debbie straightened in her seat, wincing at the spasm in her back. "You want to hire me? That's nice of you, Neil, but you see —"

"If money is the problem, I will definitely make it worth your while. I know you would rather be home with your family, so it's a big sacrifice."

"Yes, but I —"

"Believe me, Gram is the greatest person to take care of. You wouldn't have to do much, honestly. How does five hundred a day sound? Is that too low? I don't know how much private-duty nurses get. Maybe I need to scope it out a bit more so I'm giving fair wages, especially over the holidays. We're talking three twenty-four-hour days most likely, depending on what Gram needs."

Debbie nearly choked on the amount. Fifteen hundred smackaroos. That was more pay than she earned in several weeks of work. *If only* — She sighed. "Neil, I would love to do it, but I'm already working Christmas."

His cheeks pinked. He stirred in his seat, clearly flustered. "What?"

"I said, I'm working Christmas . . . at White Pines. It's my turn this year."

"You work Christmas?" His cheery countenance instantly changed to one of disappointment.

"We are scheduled to work every other Christmas. I was off last year, so it's my turn. And believe me, there's no way I can get that time off, either. It's a dead issue as far as work goes."

Neil tapped on the side of the mug. "I see." He drained the mug, then checked his watch. "Sorry, I need to get going. I have a few things to do before I see my grandmother."

Debbie winced. All the joy of the meeting quickly evaporated. Now that the air had cleared, she could see at once that he wasn't interested in her personally. He was after one thing, a nurse to take care of his grandmother. She should have known he would only take her to a coffee shop with some other motive in mind, rather than trying to get to know her. It had been this way all her life with guys, like Brad who she thought was looking her way but instead had his eye on her roommate.

Debbie swallowed down her indignation and managed to thank him for the hot chocolate. They strode out to the car in an uncomfortable silence. When he arrived at her apartment, he asked if he could check on her car.

"Don't worry — I can take care of it. Thanks anyway." Before he could respond, she gave him a brisk thank-you and darted into her apartment, shutting the door behind her. *Serves me right, getting my hopes up that a man might finally be looking my way.* He was looking for service, though a good kind of service, she had to admit. If only she didn't wrestle so much with expectations that went flying out the window at the least provocation. If only she could rely more on the plan God had for her life and not some preconceived notion. *Lord, please let me know what that plan is,* she prayed.

CHAPTER 3

Neil strode into the White Pines facility that evening without the usual exuberance that marked his step. Gram would know something was up as soon as he gave her a welcome kiss on the cheek. Despite being blind, she could read his every mood — when he had a bad day at the office or when something else ailed him. Before heading to her room, he stopped in the hall to collect his composure. He couldn't tell her the real reason for his disappointment this night: that he had failed in hiring the nurse he thought perfect for his plan to bring her home. Not only that, but he knew they had left the coffee shop on shaky ground, which didn't make him feel any better. Guess he had not been a gentleman with the lady. He had managed to get her angry after a mere sixty-minute encounter.

He glanced at the nurses walking back and forth, some greeting him with a smile.

Perhaps he would need to swallow his indignation at being chased by this colorful flock in their printed smocks and find a smiling face willing to help him with Gram. Maybe something could be gained from all the attention.

He noticed a rather tall nurse brush by him, rolling her cart of linen supplies in the direction of his grandmother's room. She turned and gave a smile before flinging back her dark blond hair.

"Hi, Neil. How's it going?"

He stopped dead in his tracks, startled that she knew his name. Had they met before?

"I'm Trish, and I've got your grandma for the evening." She pulled out her notepad with scribbles on it. "Usually I work days, but I'm pulling a little overtime tonight. Is there anything she would like this evening?"

"Actually, yes. There's something I need."

The nurse straightened, her eyes wide, as if ready to give him anything he wanted. Any other time and he would have cast the interest into the dust. Not this time. He planned to make full use of it. "I was wondering. Are you by chance off this Christmas?"

"Why, yes, I am."

"You've probably already made plans

though, right?"

"Nothing that can't be changed, of course. What's up?"

"I'm looking to hire a nurse for a few days to take care of Gram at my mother's house. It will be sort of her big Christmas gift, you might say. Would you be interested? I'll pay five hundred a day for three days."

Trish's eyes lit up. "Wow! Sure, I'd love to take care of your grandma. I pretty much know her routine, you see, since I take care of her a lot."

Neil sighed in relief, thankful he had solved his dilemma. But he couldn't settle a nagging sensation of doubt rising up within. Was that God nudging his heart? The truth be known, he wanted Debbie to be Gram's nurse. There was something about her that intrigued him. He could tell she loved the residents and wanted to care for them in the best way possible. But he couldn't have her. She was already taken — besides the fact that she was mad at him. He brushed away the feeling and offered a small smile. "Great, thanks. We'll talk over the specifics at a later date."

"Let me give you my name and cell number," she said, hurriedly writing down the information on a slip of paper before tearing it off and handing it to him. "If you want, maybe we can grab a bite to eat sometime, and you can fill me in on all the details."

"Sure," he said, stuffing the note inside the pocket of his overcoat before heading into Gram's room.

She sat in her wheelchair, humming a tune along with her favorite record. Immediately she paused, lifted her head, and smiled. "Hello, Nathaniel."

"Hi, Gram." He gave her the usual welcome kiss.

A frown settled on her face. "Oh dear, what happened? The boss give you trouble? Was it the traffic? Is it snowing out? Someone told me there may be another snowstorm soon."

"No, just gray skies out." He pulled up a chair and plunked himself down. "I have a lot on my mind."

Gram turned in her wheelchair and sniffed the air. "You went out somewhere . . . to dinner maybe? Did you eat out with a young lady? Oh, I hope so. It must get very boring eating with an old lady like me every day. You need to get out more."

Neil turned red and shifted in his seat. He never considered that his coat would carry the scent of the coffee shop. With Gram's loss of sight, her senses of smell and hear-

48

ing were quite keen. "I did go to the coffee shop," he admitted.

"Who with?"

"The nurse I helped on the road yesterday."

Gram beamed. "Wonderful! I'm so glad, Nathaniel. Did it go well?"

"Uh, not really. I mean she's nice and everything, but she's . . . uh, she's not the right one for me."

"Oh, honestly. You take a girl out once and think she's not right for you? Don't be so picky. Take her out again. For my sake."

"Gram . . . ," Neil began. A choking sensation filled his throat. "Please don't pressure me like this."

Immediately she shrank down in her wheelchair and became quiet.

Neil exhaled a loud sigh. "I'm sorry I said that. If it means so much to you, I'll take her out again. As it is, we really didn't talk about anything . . . that is, anything personal and all. It was more like a business conversation."

"Oh, give it a chance. Talk about things she likes. Be that considerate man I know and love. I'm sure she's pretty, too."

Neil considered Debbie's characteristics — her cheeks tinted pink by the wind, her blue eyes shining in the fading sunlight, the way she smiled over her cup of hot chocolate with the steam caressing her face. "I guess so. I didn't look at her in that way."

"You take her out again and then introduce me to her. I'll know if she's the right one for you."

"Gram, you're something else." He chuckled and leaned over to plant another kiss on her cheek.

"I'm more than something. I'm the one who's going to make sure you aren't alone in life." She paused then. He thought he saw tears gathering in her eyes. "To be left alone is the worst thing in life. Don't ever let it happen to you, you hear me?"

Her face at that moment remained branded within him — that hollowed look of loneliness. He was glad he had decided to arrange for her to be home for the holidays. Her words confirmed the plan — and perhaps other ideas that now began to well up in his thoughts.

Debbie was glad to leave work on time at the end of the regular day shift. She headed straight for home, thankful she didn't run the risk of seeing Neil outside the facility. The scene at the coffee shop still rubbed her nerves raw. Why did she have a problem with this anyway? Was she that desperate to be noticed by a man, like all the other nurses? Wouldn't it be better to yield such desires to God, who was quite capable of handling all the issues of her life?

Despite the emotional pain of her falling-out with Neil, at least her back seemed to be on the mend. Using a handheld mirror, Debbie could make out the bright blue and purple pattern left by the pavement. *I look like a genuine stained glass ornament,* she observed with a chuckle. The comment made her think of her Christmas decorations in storage in the basement of the small apartment building. With the few snow flurries floating around outside the window of her apartment, Debbie decided that Christmas decorating would help her forget her troubles and shift her moodiness to the joy of the upcoming holiday.

Dragging up the two boxes from storage, she rested for a bit to calm the aching in her back. Inside one box were ornaments, a music box, and a treasured Nativity set made of porcelain that immediately took a prominent position on the lamp table. The other box held an assortment of lights in one tangled ball of wire and bulbs thrown into a plastic bag. Debbie put on a CD of her favorite Christmas carols and set to work untangling the mess. *I should have done this the right way and put these strands back in their proper packaging,* she thought. But the mere idea of trying to press two hundred lights into the plastic prongs of the light boxes made her shudder. *So now I pay the price.*

Hoping not to push her frustration button, which she didn't need to do right now, she delved into a gusty rendition of a Christmas carol that drifted out of the stereo speakers. "O come, let us adore Him!" she sang. "O come, let us adore Him . . ."

"O come, let us adore Him . . . Christ the Lord," a deep voice echoed in reply.

Debbie set down the light strand. A chill swept through her. She hurried to the front door and peeked through the security hole to find Neil standing there, covered in a dusting of snow. She opened the door to the living snowman who waved his leather glove at her. "What are you doing here?"

"I've been standing here for ten minutes, listening to the carols. I figured the best way to make my entrance known was to sing along."

"I have a doorbell."

Neil shrugged. "I rang it a couple of times, but it's hard for door chimes to compete with Christmas carols. They sound like they're part of the music."

Debbie stepped aside, allowing him in. He seemed different today — joyful, interested, witty. He took off his coat and hung it over a chair to dry. "You're in the Christmas spirit, I see," he said, noting the tangled web of lights on the carpet.

"This is a royal mess, actually. Do you want to thaw out over a cup of tea? I have different flavors, like peach."

"Peach tea would be great, thanks."

Debbie entered the kitchen, fumbling to put a mug of water in the microwave. She could not recall the last time a man had graced her humble abode, except for the days of Tonya and Brad. And that was a time she'd rather forget. She dipped a teabag into the mug decorated with a bear in a nursing uniform before presenting it to Neil. He chuckled when he saw the design. "Sorry about the mug. My family thinks it's cute to give me mugs with nursing stuff on it. I get a new one every year for Christmas. I have eight of them. So you're kind of stuck with it."

"Do you plan to continue working at White Pines?"

"I guess so. There's nothing else I can do right now. I have a few college credits to my name, but no other degree." She plopped down in a chair and put her feet up on a stool. "I suppose I could go on and get a real nursing degree if I had the money and the time."

"Being a nursing assistant probably doesn't pay much, though."

She shrugged before scanning the small, one-bedroom garden apartment. "It's enough to pay the bills. Of course I can't buy new things. I get hand-me-downs from the family. Or I check out the Salvation Army store for bargains out of the bin."

"Old relics never die," he said with a nod. "Look what you get nowadays — plastic mailboxes or even blow-up furniture. There are hardly any of the old wood drawers around anymore, or stuffed armchairs that never wear out. If you can believe it, I have several old pieces inside my place."

"Really?"

"Got them at an antique store. Oh sure, my sister, Sandy, rants that I need to go contemporary. Black-and-white, I guess. But I like older stuff. It lasts much longer, even over brand-new. All one has to do nowadays is poke a pin through one of those blow-up sofas and watch it sail out the window."

Debbie suppressed a laugh. All the ideas she had conceived from their earlier meeting at the coffee shop likewise had flown out the window. She enjoyed hearing how he preferred old furniture. He certainly wasn't a stuffy, stick-your-nose-in-the-air type of person used to a lavish lifestyle. In fact, he seemed relaxed, easygoing, even tempered. *A great catch. Maybe.* She breathed out a sigh, determined not to go that way, to keep her expectations in check. One step at a time.

Neil picked up several strands of lights knotted together. Slowly, with an overwhelming patience that amazed her, he began the tedious task of untangling the lights. "I should get a few boards for you to wrap the strands around when the season is over," he remarked. "Then you won't have to deal with this again."

Debbie turned to her own set of tangled lights, hoping he didn't see the flush creeping into her face. He was being too kind. Surely there must be some other motive for this impromptu visit. "So why did you come tonight, Neil? Like I said at the coffee shop, I can't help out with your grandmother at Christmas. Switching with others is out. And if I don't show up, I'll likely be canned."

"I know. You told me." He paused, surveying the knot of lights. "This is more complicated than some of those jigsaw puzzles I used to do with Gram when I was a kid. Boy, was she a whiz at putting them together. Put me to shame." He gave a tug. "Anyway, there is a reason I came barging in here like this."

Here it comes.

"I didn't like how we left each other at the coffee shop yesterday."

Debbie stared in amazement.

"I could tell you were kind of put off by what happened. And I don't blame you." He set down the clump of lights to take a swig of the peach tea.

"Well, you didn't pull any punches. You came right out and told me the reason for splurging on the hot chocolate. I guess chocolate and hiring nurses do go together." Debbie frowned at her rising irritation. "Sorry. I guess I was put off. I was hoping it would be more of a friendly kind of thing, you know. Not that I don't understand what you were trying to do. I mean, having your grandma come home for the holidays is very noble. I'm glad you want to do it. Really."

"I'll admit that was my main goal. But looking back on it all, I realize I didn't go about it the right way. I guess, at the moment, with the idea fresh in my mind, I wanted to make it work. I think it would

56

make a great gift for Gram, something money can't buy — the idea of Christmas with the family, singing carols, watching an old Christmas movie, even roasting a chestnut or two." He looked at her with the most beautiful coffee-colored eyes she had seen in a good, long while. And she liked the small tuft of dark hair that fell over his forehead. "We all have our traditions, I guess."

"We have traditions. In my family, we always started Christmas Eve night by going to our favorite barbecue place. Then Dad insisted on taking us on a grand tour of the lighting displays. This one place had fantastic illumination with every sculpted light and plastic figurine known to mankind. They must start decorating as soon as summer is over. Dad used to do some big decorating when we were kids. You know, stringing up those lights with the megasize bulbs. He even made a model of a church once." Debbie caught herself when she realized how easily she had launched into her childhood with such eagerness. She'd never shared memories like this. With the girls at work or church, it was things like clothes or activities. This was new, different, even exciting. And especially with Neil here, soaking up every word.

"I'd like to see a big display like that sometime," he said. "And barbecue is one of my favorite foods. I would travel down to North Carolina just to get the real stuff." He returned to the lights and managed to untangle a long strand that spanned the length of the room.

Debbie pulled over the chair, ready to climb up and tack them around the windows. Neil stood below, feeding her lights as they continued to talk about Christmas memories. In an instant, everything else faded but the twinkle of lights and a handsome man helping her decorate her apartment. Could this really be happening? Well, why not? Why couldn't she relish the thought of a man helping her decorate and enjoy every bit of it? Why did she need to bask in past disappointment? The days of Brad and her roommate, Tonya, were long gone. They had their own lives. And she had hers, which was becoming even more interesting as time slipped by. Time to let go of the past and embrace the future.

They stood together, observing the lights for a moment longer, before Neil went for his coat.

"Thanks for helping me with the decorations," Debbie said.

"Hope you aren't mad anymore about the

coffee shop scene."

The flush in her face returned, hotter than ever. "I'm not mad. Not really. I just have to work out a few things, which don't have anything to do with you. Besides, I think what you're doing for your grandmother is great. I'm sure she will be thrilled by it all."

He nodded, a small smile breaking out across his face. "Maybe we can do the hot chocolate thing again sometime. Start over. Get back on track."

Debbie nodded, unable to speak. When he said good night, Debbie felt another rush of warmth invade — and not from the millions of lights now warming her home or the tea inside her tummy. It was the warmth of a good night to a sweet and considerate man. Good night and sweet dreams. And she knew who would dominate her dreams tonight.

CHAPTER 4

"Oh, Debbie, dear! Your boyfriend is calling you."

Debbie paused in midstride, carrying a tall stack of linens to make up the beds inside a room. How she wished she could just think about the meeting with Neil in her apartment a few nights ago. Instead, the craziness of work consumed her. Nearly all the residents seemed overdemanding, asking her for this or that. There were numerous accidents to clean up. Several refused to eat, forcing her to alert the head nurse, Mrs. Whitaker.

Trish looked into the room, a sardonic smile plastered on her face. Debbie knew she couldn't possibly mean Neil. No one knew about him, not that he was her boyfriend, by any means. Maybe soon he would enter that arena, if all went as planned. It did irk her some that she hadn't heard from him since the evening he helped her untangle the Christmas lights. She hoped they weren't at another impasse. She thought the evening had gone pretty well. And he had left it open-ended, with another coffee or chocolate meeting to come in the near future.

Suddenly Debbie heard a loud voice echoing down the hallway. "Shore up that line! Get to the top of the ridge on the double. I know the Germans are coming. We'll get murdered standing here. Move on out!"

Trish leaned against the door frame. "Mrs. Whitaker asked if you could calm dear Harold down. I guess you have a knack for that kind of thing. He probably thinks you remind him of his girlfriend from the 1940s or something."

Debbie gritted her teeth and plunked the stack of linens on a bed. How she disliked Trish's demeaning ways. She could certainly think up a good retort, were it not for Christian virtue that made her bridle her tongue. She prayed for patience as she brushed by Trish to hear the racket that grew louder as she approached. When she peeked inside Harold's room, she found the poor man sliding halfway out of his wheelchair. His hair stood up like a wild man, his face unshaven. She exhaled loudly. Harold was Trish's patient, no doubt. He bore all the telltale signs.

Debbie came around behind and hoisted him up so he sat properly in his chair. "What's the matter, Harold?"

He looked back at her with a wild look in his eyes. "What are you doing? Don't you know there's a war going on? Duck down 'fore the enemy sees you."

Debbie calmly walked over to the night-stand and took a comb out of the drawer. "Harold, we've had these talks before. World War II has been over for sixty years."

"What? That's impossible. I'd be an old man if the Great War ended sixty years ago."

Debbie bit her lip to keep from laughing. He did have a sense of humor, despite his memory lapses.

"In fact, if the war's been over sixty years, I'd be in my eighties at least, and I'm only twenty-four."

He was absolutely right. Debbie marveled at the way Harold could make rationalizations like these, even if he did say other irrational things. But to his mind, everything made perfect sense and she was the one off her rocker. Maybe a little reality check might set things straight and clear his thoughts. She wheeled him into the bathroom and to the mirror hanging low on the wall. "See, Harold? You're not in your twenties anymore. You're a man of wisdom."

He said nothing but stared. She heard a sniffle and looked down to find tears glistening on his cheeks. "Get me out of here," he ordered. Debbie hurriedly wheeled him back into the room. He continued to sit there, staring, the tears drifting down.

Her lower lip trembled. Regret instantly filled her. For all she knew, Harold found comfort in his youthful identity, and in an instant, she had shattered it. "I'm so sorry, Harold. I thought it would be good for you to see that you aren't a young man anymore."

He only turned away from her to stare at the wall. Debbie twisted her face in dismay. What did it hurt if Harold wanted to believe he was still young? If it made him happy and made him feel as if he still had a life to live, even in his advanced years, then why not? Instead, she had ripped it all away from him.

Debbie shook her head and retreated to the hall to find Trish standing just outside the door, a wide grin painted on her face. "Bravo! What a show. Did you really think crazy old Harold would want to see himself in the mirror?"

Debbie began to stew. "I don't know. I thought it was worth trying to get him to see reality."

"Honey, none of these people here think they're old. They all think they're swinging singles from way back when hoopskirts were in fashion."

"You're a little off. They didn't wear hoop-skirts in the 1940s. Anyway, maybe you could clean Harold up a little more. And he could use a shave."

"So now you're the high-and-mighty nurse who knows everything? Where is your advanced degree that says you can order me around? Huh?"

Debbie blew out a sigh and hurried off to the room where the linens still sat on the unmade bed. She shouldn't have opened her mouth about Trish's untidy habits. Now the whole floor would know what she said and be on her case about it. Debbie shook her head. She needed to talk to Mrs. Whita-ker about Trish anyway. The woman shouldn't even be working here, considering the way she treated the residents. Not that Debbie had seen Trish do anything hor-rendous like the stories she had heard about abuse in these places. But the way Trish kept her charges looking so untidy or offered snide remarks, in Debbie's eyes, was akin to maltreatment. Even so, after being here eight years, Debbie knew well what could happen if she did make waves. Trish had plenty of friends on staff who could make Debbie's life miserable. And others before her had been chased away for littler things.

Making the bed in rapid fashion, Debbie walked down the corridor and paused by Harold's door. He was sitting better in his wheelchair. His clothes were neat, but he still looked listless. His eyes stared blankly from his unshaven face. Debbie glanced up the hall and, seeing no sign of Trish, ventured back inside. "Let's get a shave, Harold. Spiff you up a little for all the girls."

"Huh? What for? I'm just an old geezer. Everyone tells me I'm old, that I look old, that I am old."

"I'm sorry about what happened, Harold. Please, can I give you a shave?" She held up the electric razor.

He said nothing as she approached. Only when she turned on the razor did he flinch. His extremities began to quake. Fear was clearly spelled out in his eyes that grew all the more wild. "We're gonna have to get off these boats," he said to her. "But I see the bullets. The enemy's already firing at us. But we gotta head for the beach anyway. There's no turning back."

"Where are we headed, Harold?"

"To Omaha, of course. We're supposed to

take Omaha Beach. Me and Sam, we're going together. We trained together. Got on the same landing craft together. We're both real scared, too. He's my best friend, you know."

Debbie recalled the movies she had seen about that awful day at Normandy on the shores of France. She remembered thumbing through her father's multitude of coffee-table books about World War II. But here sat a man who had witnessed, firsthand, a time period that lived in infamy. Why hadn't she even considered it before trying to make him see the reality of living in the present day?

"Sam got sick to his stomach," Harold went on. "Seasickness, I guess. He used his helmet as a bucket until I told him to just lean over the side of the boat. Then we heard the bullets. He was tugging on my jacket. I said there weren't nothing to fear, that the enemy couldn't hit the broadside of a barn."

"It must have been real scary," she said, running the electric shaver around his chin. He lifted his head higher so she could shave his neck.

"When the boys started dying, it was. They died right in front of me. One by one." Suddenly his shoulders began to heave. The tears bubbled over. "They died. Sam died. Everyone in my company died, except me. I was on my own. I didn't know anyone on the beach. I was all alone with bullets all around."

Debbie stood there, mesmerized by the story. Just then his grisly hand took hers. His skin was dry, the veins crisscrossing the top of his hand like the streets on a road map. "Don't ever be alone, young lady. Being alone with the enemy closing in is the worst thing in life."

Debbie managed to pat his hand before putting back the razor. Just as quickly, Harold lapsed into a quiet pensiveness, staring straight ahead. She looked at him, thinking of all the scenes that replayed over and over in his mind like a rerun with no end. She felt sorry for him.

Debbie ventured to the nurses' station to check the assignment sheet and found Trish loitering there along with two cohorts, Meg and Natasha. When they saw her, they gathered together like a flock of hens and began their clucking. Debbie refused to embrace the old fear left over from the high school days of students talking behind her back, though she was certain the nurses were doing just that.

"So old Harold has you wrapped around

his finger, eh?" Trish said with a huge smile painted on her face. The other two nurses giggled.

"Why don't you leave him alone? He doesn't have long to live in this world anyway. No one here does. They have to spend the rest of their existence here, so we should make it as nice as possible for them. We're the only real family they have."

"They're not my family," Natasha announced in disgust, staring at her set of purple polished fingernails. "I'm only in this place until I find a better job."

"The problem with Debbie is that she thinks these people are her pets," Trish added.

"Actually, Trish, it's you who treats them like dogs," she muttered and headed back down the hall.

Trish followed. "Excuse me? What did you say?"

Debbie felt the heat rise in her neck even as she tried to look the other way.

"If you have something to say, say it to my face."

Debbie whirled. "Okay. Leave Harold alone. And don't call him names. If anything, he should be treated like a hero. A lot of men like Harold bled and died so you could stand there and say the things you do."

Trish hooted. "Honey, no one died for me, 'specially little old Harold who doesn't even know what planet he's on."

Jesus died for you, Debbie thought, but this was hardly the time or atmosphere to delve into her heartfelt beliefs. "People need to look more at history. See what soldiers have accomplished and the freedoms they have won for us. Our country would be a much different place without their sacrifices."

"Huh? What are you talking about?"

Debbie could see this conversation was going nowhere fast. She excused herself to check on several patients, with Trish glaring at her as she hurried down the hall. Ducking inside a linen alcove, she steadied herself. Maybe Neil was right. Maybe it was time to look for another job, not only to bring in more money but also to escape people like Trish. . . .

. . . that is, until she heard a voice shouting at some unseen German enemy invading White Pines. Down the hall she went, with a strength greater than herself. If no one else on earth needed her, Harold did and maybe Elvina, too. And that was enough to keep her feet entrenched in this place, at least for now.

Despite trying to turn things around and salvage the day at White Pines, Debbie left work feeling depressed about where she was going in life. She wondered if her faith was at all evident to the staff and patients. For certain, the staff disliked her. If it weren't for the residents like Elvina and Harold and the relationships she'd fostered with them, she might be tempted to move away from this area altogether. What was keeping her here anyway? None of her family lived here. They made their home in northern Virginia where her father still negotiated the nightmare of Interstate 66 at rush hour, trucking it into Washington, D.C., every day. For herself, Debbie couldn't stand the thought of working in some metropolitan city that extended far beyond the borders of the District of Columbia. She made a big break after two years of community college, venturing as far south as possible, back to country living with less stress — or so she thought. She took a six-month nursing assistant course at a community college, then went looking for a job. Settling here in the foothills of the Blue Ridge in the tiny hamlet of Fincastle, she found something about the area that she enjoyed. Maybe the hilly surroundings with the grand scope of the Blue Ridge spanning the distant horizon. Fincastle also had quaint homes, some dating back generations, and held its own unique niche in history as the hometown of Julia Hancock, the wife of William Clark of the famous Lewis and Clark expedition. It was a nice area. But was it enough to keep her here, especially with what she had to endure at work and beyond?

Okay, quit throwing yourself a glorified pity party. She entered her car, thankful to have her set of wheels back — finally. The very next day after untangling the Christmas lights and sharing peach tea with Neil at her apartment, Hank's Auto Service called to say the car was ready. And the price was far cheaper than what she had originally been quoted. *Did Neil have a hand in me getting my car back, I wonder?* The mere thought made her feel better.

Driving to the store in Daleville to pick up a few groceries, Debbie made the decision to look on the bright side of things. God had placed her at White Pines for a reason. She felt good about being around the residents and caring for their needs, both physically and emotionally. Maybe the attacks from people like Trish were confirmations that she was doing the right thing, even if she felt beaten down by them at times.

Debbie hadn't been cruising the store aisle more than fifteen minutes when she heard a familiar male voice whistling an old-time Christmas carol. Neil stood in the aisle with his own shopping basket in hand that held a can of shortbread cookies, a package of mints, and a bag of lozenges. She couldn't help but laugh, first at the idea of running into him in the same aisle of a huge grocery store, and second at the items he had chosen.

"Hi, Neil. Great start to the dinner you have planned," she teased.

He spun around. "Debbie, hi! So you like my choices, do you?"

"It's certainly unique."

He acknowledged his basket. "I plan to start off the evening fare with an appetizer of mints. Nothing like a sugar high to get you off on the right footing. Then a main course of shortbread cookies. And for dessert, assorted throat lozenges to cool the palate."

Debbie laughed long and loud, a freeing kind of laugh where the frustrations of life took flight in a hurry. "Mine isn't much better," she acknowledged, looking down at the contents of her basket — chocolate-covered ice cream bars, hot cocoa mix, and a stick of deodorant.

"I see chocolate. Is someone having another bad day?"

His observation sent tears springing to her eyes.

His voice softened. "Is your back still hurting you? I think you'd better have a doctor take a look at it. My sister once hurt her back and never got it checked. It bothers her even still. Sometimes she's in bed for a few days. She can't lift anything over twenty pounds."

"No, it's not that." Debbie rested the basket on a display of canned fruit. "What can I say? Life these days is definitely making me want to mix up a batch of lemonade. In fact, I'd better go get some."

"Put your stuff back," he ordered. "Time for that second round of hot chocolate I promised you."

She gazed at him. A smirk played on his lips, offset by the seriousness in his eyes.

"Guess I should. The ice cream bars aren't going to make it home anyway. But you can still buy your exotic dinner for that special someone."

He laughed. "Meet you in the front of the store."

Twenty minutes later, they were sitting at

the same table they had occupied the week before, with two cups of chocolate before them. When Neil got to the punch line of a joke he'd heard at work, Debbie laughed and blew on the steam before taking a sip. She had to admit this encounter was much better than the first. Especially since Neil appeared sensitive to her woes and expressed a desire to help. She delved into the shortened version of the day's struggles, including Harold's battle with Normandy versus the twenty-first century and the callous mistake she'd made in showing him his reflection in the bathroom mirror.

"There's nothing wrong with trying to point an elderly gentleman to reality," he said.

"But you should have seen the reactions of my fellow coworkers. They thought it was some joke, like it's a scream to poke fun at an older man."

He rolled his eyes. "I can tell you for a fact that most of them don't even know what planet they're on. They don't want to be working there, and it shows. And for sure, they don't care about the residents the way you do."

"How do you know I care?"

He leaned over the table. "Is that a trick question? I can hear it in your voice. You're concerned you might have upset this Harold fellow by showing him his image in the mirror. And then your interest in his past. Seems to me, these days, no one wants to know about another's past, present, or future."

She took another sip. "Okay. So what about your past, present, and future?"

He hesitated at first. "Well, let's just say my past is better left right where it is. My present, I will have to wait for Christmas to see. Probably socks and underwear. And only God really knows the future, if we are patient enough to wait and find out."

Again a funny smirk spread across his face, this time accompanied by a twinkle in his eyes. So this Neil did have a bit of humor about him. But Debbie sensed there were other things left unspoken, as well. She had to admit, his comment about the past stirred up her curiosity to know more. But she wouldn't pry. She would wait.

"And you?" he asked.

"I grew up in northern Virginia in the fast lane. Or rather the HOV lane. My present would be a cruise to Alaska. And my future is like yours. Whatever God wants." She bowed her head then, feeling the warmth in her cheeks, even as he stared at her. She could sense a bond already forming. It amazed her. And here she thought she wasn't cut out for love. Maybe God was trying to show her otherwise. "Anyway, I'll get through this time somehow. He's been faithful to help me every day."

"That's right. And you are meant right now to work at White Pines, even if it gets a little tough. Just keep doing what you're supposed to do and don't worry about everyone else. We're told to take care of our neighbor. 'Love one another,' as the Bible says. And I hate to say it, but that includes those who treat us like junk sometimes, such as your coworkers, for example."

"Easier said than done," she mumbled, thinking of Trish.

"It's happened to me. I had a coworker of the higher-ups give me extra caseloads because he didn't like me, or so I thought. I sat there and wondered if maybe he had a falling-out with someone at home. A bad family life. Disappointment. If you can put the person in a different light, it helps."

"You need to come to work with me and be my conscience. Like Jiminy Cricket in *Pinocchio*. You can even wear a top hat and a red umbrella to go along with your black coat."

Neil laughed. "Debbie, I think you already have things figured out. Just hang tough.

Take each day, one at a time. It's all any of us can do, you know."

As long as her days were filled with him, washed down with cups of hot chocolate, she had no doubt they would be good days. She left the shop feeling renewed. Sure, life's troubles were still there in one form or another, but at least they seemed smaller. Even insignificant. And that was a welcome change.

CHAPTER 5

Debbie awoke the next morning feeling better than she had in ages. Something about her encounter with Neil put everything in a new light. She decided to employ some of his wisdom to her situation and see what transpired. She would think of Trish, Natasha, and all the rest as women wrapped up in a perpetual fog of unhappiness, unable to see anything clearly. She would consider them as Jesus would — lost people who needed love not confrontation. Though it would be difficult to assert such love when following behind Trish, picking up after her, and tending to the care she'd left undone, Debbie would do her best.

With her new attitude in place, Debbie found the day proceeding smoothly. The fact that Trish also had the day off didn't hurt matters. Mrs. Whitaker did not assign Debbie to Elvina's wing but to the other wing that included Harold's room. He perked up when he saw her, smiling a tooth-less grin for the first time that she could recall. Debbie took her time pampering him a little, giving him a thorough shave, scouring around for some aftershave lotion to smooth on his face, and dressing him in a new sport shirt.

"Did you ever get married, Harold?"

"No. Never had a girl. Sam did, but I didn't. He talked about her all the time. His Liv, he called her."

"Liv? Was that short for Olivia?"

"Don't know. When he went off to fight, Sam left her and the boy behind. He told me all about them, how he was gonna marry her and be a real father to that little boy. He told me . . . told me to . . ." Harold stopped then, as if a switch had been turned off. A strange look distorted his rough features.

"Harold?"

He began to tremble and then looked off in the distance. "Hey, you there! What are you doing out of line? Get back in line right now, or the major's gonna have it in for you."

Debbie sighed. Once more he had lapsed into that strange battle state of sixty-some-odd years ago. When she tried to coax him back again, he refused. For a man who sometimes did not delve in reality, Harold had a knack for stubbornness. Sometimes she sensed pride holding him in that time period. Or, perhaps Harold found comfort in a wartime frame of mind, as if the present day proved more painful than D-day. Why he would think that, she had no idea.

"Debbie, I need a favor." Mrs. Whitaker stood in the doorway with the medication cart. She was of the "old school" of nursing, clad in her pure white dress with the nursing button of her alma mater prominently displayed, white hose, and white nursing shoes. Debbie was thankful the nursing assistants could wear colorful tops and white clogs. Her favorite smock this time of year was the one with holly and berries sprinkled across the fabric. And in January, Debbie liked to wear one covered in flowers to remind her of the coming spring.

"Can you work overtime tonight? I had two call in sick for the evening shift, and we're running short. If you can work until seven, that would be great."

Debbie quickly agreed. *More time on my mission field,* she decided. She would love to have Neil tagging along with her, telling her what to do, being her encouragement, lifting her head up when it sometimes sank to her chest in dejection. Then she realized Neil was merely a messenger. God was the source of her encouragement — her head lifter.

The rest of the day went smoothly with these thoughts singing in her head. Even when most of the day shift went home and Debbie remained behind, she felt light on her feet as if she had barely worked an eight-hour shift already. When Debbie got a break, she decided to pay Elvina a visit. Debbie came in whistling, hoping to put on a record for her and hear her sing. Elvina sat in her wheelchair by her bedside, staring toward the door with her hands folded on her lap as if waiting for something. "Hi, Elvina, it's Debbie."

"Oh, it's my little nurse. How are you, dear? I haven't seen you in such a long time. Are you working this evening?"

Elvina, with her eyes blinded to everything around her, had never literally *seen* Debbie, but Debbie knew what she meant. "Yes, for a few hours. For some reason, I've been assigned the other hall the last week or so. Do you want me to put on a record for you?"

"No, thank you. I'm waiting for Nathaniel to come. He's late today. I already hear the dinner carts coming down the hallway."

Debbie looked at her watch. "It's 5:30."

"Tsk, tsk. He always comes at 5:00. Must be there was a lot of traffic."

"I'm sure he will be here." Suddenly it dawned on her that she would get the opportunity to see this infamous grandson of Elvina's, the one who had given her the record player, the one everyone on staff raved about. She wondered why she had always missed seeing the man when working overtime. Oh well. Tonight, the mystery of Elvina's Nathaniel would be solved. Debbie chuckled to herself until she glanced at Elvina's nightstand. Sitting on top was a tin of shortbread cookies that looked vaguely familiar.

"What are you up to?" Elvina asked.

Leave it to Elvina to sense something was up. She had eyes in the back of her head. "Oh, nothing. Just wondering if you've eaten any of the cookies yet?"

"Are you hungry? Help yourself. I was going to ask the nurses if they would like to have them. To be honest, why Nathaniel thinks I should have cookies, I don't know. Yes, I do have a sweet tooth, but I'm afraid you sweet things will hurt your backs trying to get me out of bed if I keep eating cookies and candy."

Debbie wondered if it would be too presumptuous to open Elvina's drawer and check for throat lozenges. Just then she heard the nurses' station paging her. She hurried off, not giving it another thought until she returned half an hour later. Debbie went to check on Elvina and see if her grandson had made it in. She peeked in and saw a man with a rugged build sitting by Elvina's wheelchair. His back was to her, but she plainly saw the shocks of dark hair. He and Elvina were laughing. Debbie sucked in her breath. She didn't want to give the appearance of being overzealous as so many of the staff had been known to do. She decided simply to stride in, in a businesslike fashion. Maybe she could take the two dinner trays while stealing a quick glance.

Lifting her head high, Debbie marched in. "Let me get those trays out of your way," she declared, swiping up the trays.

"Oh, Nathaniel, this is the sweet nurse I was telling you about," Elvina said.

Nathaniel turned. They stared at each other.

"Neil?"

"Debbie?"

She burst out laughing, in keeping with the season of unpredictable joy. The surprise tickled her all the way to her toes inside her white clogs, as did the delightful smile erupting on Neil's face. "My day is complete."

"Mine, too."

Neil couldn't believe that the nurse his grandmother adored turned out to be Debbie, though he wasn't totally surprised. Debbie had a fondness for the residents that was unmistakable. He could tell right away the two of them shared a special bond, which he hoped to share with Debbie, as well. When Gram launched into how Debbie made her feel beautiful with makeup and combing her hair, Neil cast a smile in Debbie's direction. He was getting more impressed by the minute.

"Debbie cares, Gram. She's a great person."

She sat up straighter in her chair. "You know her, Nathaniel?"

A blush filled Debbie's face, making her appear all the more attractive — though he thought her attractive anyway, with the way her soft brown hair lay on her shoulders. Recalling her hunched over that hot chocolate, the steam in her face, he couldn't help but stare. The holly and berries printed on her nursing smock, coupled with her cheerful countenance, brightened his day — especially a cold and dreary December one like today.

"This is simply wonderful," Gram cooed.

"Nathaniel has been telling me all about a nurse who had fallen in the road. Was it you, Debbie? You're still here, aren't you?"

"I'm right here, Elvina. Yes, I did take a fall about a week or two ago. If it weren't for your grandson, I might have been turned into a human waffle under the wheels of a delivery truck."

Gram picked up Neil's hand and gave a squeeze. A tear or two trickled out of her eyes. "This is so sweet, I can't help but cry," she confessed. "How I prayed you would find a nice lady to settle down with. I just know you two are perfect for each other."

Neil glanced at Debbie who was using a fork from one of the trays to trace an imaginary line across the bedside table. He could tell that she was trying to decide how to take all this. The truth be known, Neil had been thinking quite a bit about Debbie. He had that trip back and forth from Roanoke, with plenty of time for contemplating and planning. Of course, one could hardly plan out a future relationship. That fell in God's department. Neil didn't want to make a mess of things. But he did like the feeling he got whenever he was around Debbie. And presto, here she was — caring for Gram, no less!

Debbie picked up the trays. "I guess I'd

better get these into the cart before the cafeteria guys roll it away."

"Let me get the other tray," Neil offered. Gram looked on, grinning from ear to ear, as if she had planned this all out and everything was proceeding on cue. The whole notion made him suddenly bashful. The words became tangled in his throat as he walked a few paces behind Debbie down the hallway. At the large metal cart, they each slid in their respective trays.

"So you come here every evening to eat with Elvina, I mean, your grandmother?" Debbie asked.

"Most evenings."

"Small world."

"Small facility." He nodded toward the hallway that branched off into another part of the building. "Who would've thought you would be working on this floor."

"Actually I'm only here another hour or so. I usually work days, but they needed an extra hand until seven."

"I'll probably be leaving around then. I'd offer you a ride, but I take it you have your car back, right?"

Debbie nodded. He wondered then if they should do something after her shift was over. What does one do on a Wednesday evening? He'd already had his dinner. He didn't know if she'd eaten or not. Maybe get a pizza? That sounded like teenybopper stuff. They had done the coffee shop scene, even run into each other at the grocery store. He wasn't about to invite himself over to her apartment again. Downtown Fincastle offered little in the way of entertainment, and meeting at the shopping plaza at Daleville seemed lame. Roanoke held many possibilities but was too far out of the way for a midweek outing. He considered it for a time until he saw Debbie staring inquisitively.

"Something wrong?"

"No. Just thinking."

"Well, I have to check on the other residents. Have a good visit."

He sighed, wishing he had come up with something, but let the idea slide for the time being. Instead, he returned to his grandmother to find her sitting there quietly, looking distant, as if in deep thought. "You okay, Gram?"

"Oh, of course. Just thinking about you two gets me thinking about my sweetheart when I was young."

Neil grimaced. He was never good at talking to her about Grandpa Joe, who had passed away two years ago. Gram seemed to take it well when she learned her husband had died in his sleep. But comments like this always threw him for a loop, wondering what to say or how to react.

"My long-lost love." She straightened then, her gray blue eyes growing deeper in color to a near navy blue. "You never saw what he looked like. A pity."

The remark puzzled him. "Sure I have. Plenty of times."

"No, you haven't. I don't think your mother has a single picture of him anywhere. No one does that I know of. Your father was too small to have pictures. He was only three when his dad left. I don't think he gave him a picture, but he should have."

What is she talking about? This was getting more confusing by the minute. Of course there were pictures of Grandpa Joe. He began to panic, wondering if Gram was having some kind of memory lapse. Maybe some disease lay lurking there for a long time, like that dreaded Alzheimer's disease, and now it had surfaced. "Gram, I've seen many pictures of Grandpa. Mom has them sitting there on the mantel."

She shook her head. "If only I knew how to say these things right, but I don't. I do wish you knew him, Nathaniel. You remind me of him. The way you greet people. The way you treat a lady — like helping my little nurse when she fell. He was chivalrous. He would help anyone."

"Gram, I know it was hard to lose Grandpa, but he's in heaven. He was a fine Christian man."

"I don't know where he is," she said hollowly. "I don't know if he's alive or dead. I wish I did. If there were one wish I could have, it would be to see him one last time. If only he could tell me why he wrote just one letter and why I never heard from him again. If only I could tell him about your father — what a fine young man he turned out to be, and then the fine children he had, like you. He would be so proud."

Neil stared, his hands sinking deeper into his pockets. None of this was making any sense. He whirled and walked out into the hallway, scanning the nurses' station. Everyone was gone, probably involved in evening care to ready the residents for the night. He needed to talk to someone, a doctor maybe, someone who could tell him if his grandmother was suffering a mental defect. Debbie would know. She knew Gram like the back of her hand. At least he hoped she did. He walked down the hall, peeking in each room until he found her.

"Hi, Neil." She paused. "Is something

wrong?"

He waited until she came out into the hallway. "It's Gram. Something's not right. She keeps talking about Grandpa like she hasn't seen him in thirty years. He just died a couple of years ago. And now she's asking to see him again."

Debbie sighed. "I'm sorry, Neil. Sometimes a mind can wander in the evening. It's just temporary. She'll be better in the morning."

"I've never heard her say these things before. She says there are no pictures of him either and that I've never even seen what he looks like. Debbie, I have a picture of Grandpa Joe sitting on my bureau at home. I knew him very well."

"I don't know what to say, Neil. If you want, I can try and talk to her."

"No. It might make her more confused and upset. I just wish I knew what to do." Neil strode away, staring at the floor tiles. It had finally happened. His dear grandmother had gone senile, and when he least expected it. Looking at his watch, he decided to call it an evening before anything else absurd came forth. Heading back to her room, he paused in the doorway to study her. She appeared sweet and innocent, so lucid really, talking about a long-lost love, her sweetheart, as if he were a real person. Maybe he was, in her mind.

When Neil walked into the room, her head turned. "I thought you had left without saying good-bye. That's not like you."

"Gram, I'm worried."

"About what?" She said it as if he were the one going senile.

"What you said about Grandpa Joe. It doesn't make any sense."

"I wasn't talking about Joe. Dear Joe. I know he's in heaven, bless his heart. I just wondered what happened to your other grandfather."

My other grandfather? "What? You mean my mom's dad?"

She waved at him. "No, no, no. Your father's father. Your real grandfather. Oh, never mind. It's getting late. Can you send for Debbie? I need to get ready for bed. And you need to go home before it gets too late." She turned her wrinkled cheek toward him, waiting for him to bestow the nightly ritual of a kiss on her cheek. He obliged, only to have her pinch his own in an affectionate way.

"Don't worry about things. I'm fine."

"I'll try not to," Neil managed to say.

Leaving White Pines that night, he felt like he was walking in a daze. *My dad had another father who wasn't Grandpa Joe?* If so, he knew nothing about him. Could it be something that had been hidden away all these years, only to come forth now? He kicked up a stone. And why now, when other things were on his mind. He didn't need this disruption in his life. He was considering things that he had never considered before: being together with Debbie, believing life might finally — at age thirty-five — be coming together for him. Why did this have to come out now?

CHAPTER 6

Neil drove home in a cloud of confusion and questioning. Not even the flashing Christmas lights in the windows or the outlandish blow-up snowmen and Santas in the front lawns made him turn his head. Instead, he only stared at the road ahead. *What other man is Gram talking about?* He hoped the cold night air, blowing on him through the car vent, would wake him up to reality. Maybe this was just a temporary lapse in Gram's thinking and everything would be back to normal when he saw her next. He gripped the steering wheel as he drove onto Interstate 81, heading for Roanoke. Maybe he should call the floor tomorrow and let Gram know he was under the weather and wouldn't be in. That would give them both time to clear their heads and set things straight. He needed it. Right now his felt like a fog machine had been turned on inside. He couldn't even see.

Maybe I should talk to Debbie or the head nurse and find out if they've switched her medication. Once, they had given Gram a new sleeping pill so she could rest. That night, she became completely delirious, climbing out of bed and trying to walk around the room. She nearly fell. Maybe they had given her a new pill, and now the side effects were showing up as a delusion of some man contrived in her mind, some sweetheart, someone she even insisted was his true grandfather, of all things.

His cell phone played a tune, interrupting his thoughts. He struggled for it, buried under gloves and some papers from work. Looking at the number, he saw it was White Pines. *This is it.* They were going to tell him that his grandmother had indeed taken a turn for the worse, that her mind and emotions were completely off the wall, that everything he knew and loved about her was gone.

"Neil, it's Debbie."

He tensed. "Don't tell me there's something else wrong with Gram."

"Nothing's wrong. I'm just concerned about you."

"How did you get this number?"

"Off Elvina's — I mean, your grandmother's — chart."

"It's good you called, actually. I need you to find out for me if they have her on some kind of new medication. Something that may be giving her hallucinations."

"I can ask the charge nurse, but I don't think she's on anything new. Neil, I wish that you would tell me what's going on."

He gripped the tiny phone until his hand went numb. "It's just that she's talking about things that make no sense. Like her mind has snapped or something."

A pause came over the line. "Neil, I've been with her the last twenty minutes. In fact, I'm even staying until nine to make sure she's okay. She seems completely lucid to me when I'm with her. But I can tell she's worried about you. She thinks she upset you."

An understatement, to say the least. She might as well have thrown a bucket of ice water on me. "I just don't know what to think with the way she is carrying on about my grandfather."

"It's that time of year," Debbie's soothing voice came over the phone. "People tend to think more about loved ones. They get to reminiscing."

"You don't seem the least bit concerned."

"No. And neither should you. Just pray about it. I'm sure when you see her tomorrow everything will be better."

"I'm not coming in tomorrow. I think I'll lay low and wait for this to pass." He paused before adding, "Actually, when she found out about you and me, that's what brought this on — all this talk about some sweetheart. So I think we also need to cool it for a while."

A pause came over the line. "Exactly what is it I'm supposed to cool?"

He could hear her vexation on the rise but thought little of it. "Just tell Gram that we aren't interested in each other, okay? Tell her we just happened to bump into each other, that kind of thing. We hardly know each other anyway, so it doesn't matter."

He heard a gasp followed by, "Sure. Whatever you want."

Then silence.

Great, Neil thought. *She hung up. Well, what am I supposed to do? The reason Gram got off on this whole sweetheart idea was because she thought Debbie and I were going out. All I want to do is push Gram back into the reality of her husband and my grandfather named Joe, the only grandfather I've ever known.*

Neil felt no better when he arrived in Roanoke. Everything looked so cheerful with white lights decorating the office buildings. Some houses were decked out in so many lights that the air traffic in the skies above would have no problem zeroing in on Roanoke. But his mood right now didn't match the gleaming decorations. Nor was he in the mood to head for his lonely apartment, even if the guy in the condo next door would likely call him up, looking to play a computer game.

Instead, he drove to the suburbs of Roanoke. Soon he was passing places where he learned to ride a bike with training wheels, sold oranges and magazines to neighbors for school fund-raising projects, played street hockey with the neighborhood kids. At the end of the cul-de-sac stood the family home, a modest one-level ranch over a basement. And here, he stopped.

"Neil!" his mother exclaimed when she answered the door. "I wasn't expecting you."

"I should have called first, instead of just showing up on your doorstep."

She gave him a kiss. "I'm always glad to have you drop by. No one seems to do it anymore. Everyone's too busy."

The television blasted from the family room. Neil figured the chatter of the tube probably kept her company. Thankfully this wasn't her night to be with her friends at the quilting club, the Red Hat Club, or any number of her other clubs that kept her occupied. When he thought about it, he realized he should probably come by more often for a visit. "Have you heard from Sandy or Dick?" Neil asked.

A smile broke out across her face. "Yes. They're planning to be here for Christmas. Isn't that wonderful? I'll have all my kids together. I'll bake all your favorite cookies. You can start a fire in the fireplace. I haven't used the thing since the last time you all were here; was it Thanksgiving a few years back? We'll have a wonderful time."

"Great to hear, Mom. Anyway, there are a few things I need to talk about concerning Christmas."

She led the way to the living room, where they sat down. All at once, his eyes fell on twin portraits of his paternal grandmother and grandfather. Gram and Grandpa Joe. There they were, as plain as day. Maybe he should ask Mom if he could borrow the pictures to give Gram a reality check.

"You look like something's on your mind," she observed. "Have you had dinner? I can make you up something quick."

"I ate with Gram."

"Oh yes, of course. How is she doing? I need to go see her soon."

"Look, I went to see her tonight, and she

was saying some pretty strange things."

She straightened in her chair, a look of distress distorting her features. "Oh dear. Don't tell me she's going downhill. I've heard people say that the holidays are hard on older people. I understand because the holidays are hard on me, too."

"Mom, this may sound strange, but tonight Gram was talking about another man. Some sweetheart of hers from long ago. She said no one probably has ever seen him, that there were no pictures. And she denied that this was Grandpa Joe. Do you have any idea what she's talking about?"

Her eyes widened. She shifted in her seat and looked off in the direction of the miniature Christmas tree sitting on a table. "Neil, you know older people. I'm sure it was some old boyfriend from long ago." She added in a high-pitched voice, "Though I don't know why on earth she would mention him. She had a wonderful marriage with your grandfather."

"Which grandfather?"

She turned pale. "What are you talking about? Grandpa Joe, of course." She pointed to the picture.

"That's not what Gram said. She called this man my other grandfather. She said Dad had a different father. And he wasn't

Grandpa Joe."

Her jaw tightened. "Neil, honestly. Your grandmother is over eighty. She's already lost her sight and her mobility. Who knows what's happening to her mind? I'm sure she just came up with this because she's feeling lonely. I know what it's like to be lonely, even though your father would have wanted me to remarry. But I couldn't do it, even though I came close. He was my one and only."

"So there isn't anything to what she says? This is purely old age and nothing else?"

She began to fidget before standing and walking into the kitchen. "Do you want something to drink?"

"Sure, thanks."

He ventured to the doorway, observing her pour soda out of a two-liter bottle. He was never good at picking up on emotional responses, but clearly his mother seemed troubled by something. Maybe his grandmother wasn't so crazy after all. Maybe there was something slowly being brought to light. When Neil took the glass of soda from his mother, she refused to make eye contact. He drank it down, wishing he could muster some time to scout around the house for clues. But what clue was he supposed to find? He didn't even know where to begin. And Mom wasn't being helpful at all.

He thought of broaching the other subject, his once glorious idea of inviting Gram to spend Christmas with them. That had to take a backseat right now. One stress point at a time. He had to get this ironed out first.

The rest of the evening was consumed by the mundane. What his brother and sister were doing. His nieces, his sister Sandy's kids, and what Mom planned to buy them for Christmas. Dick's new job. He wondered if his siblings were privy to this mystery surrounding an alternate grandfather, if they had heard of such a thing or knew of a skeleton hanging in the family closet.

He picked up his coat, telling his mother he had to go.

"Neil, please forget about what Elvina said," she said, staring in concern. "You're making yourself upset over nothing. Let it go."

"I wish I could, Mom. But I think there may be more here than meets the eye." He made for the door.

She nearly ran to him, putting her hand on his arm. Her lower lip quivered, and tears welled in her eyes. "Neil, I'm begging you. Let it go. Whatever it is, it's not worth rehashing."

He carried the memory of his mother's troubled face into the cold winter's night. Something was afoot. Something strange. A secret kept under wraps for years — until now. How could he possibly let this go? This had to do with his flesh and blood, after all. His lineage. His heritage. He had a right to know the truth.

As soon as he got into the car, Neil picked up his cell phone. He wasted no time contacting his sister to tell her what was happening.

She only laughed. "Neil, Gram's an old lady. Let her have some fun with her memories or whatever."

He grimaced. How typical of Sandy to make light of something this serious. She always said older people made her feel uncomfortable. She couldn't understand why he would want to spend evenings with their grandmother when he could be out on the town, living it up. For all he knew, she had never put one foot in White Pines. "I hardly would call this fun. It's serious. You and I may have some grandfather other than Grandpa Joe. Our father's father could be a stranger we never knew existed."

"Even if we did, he's long gone by now. What's the big deal? So what if Gram had a lover before Grandpa Joe and they shacked up together. That's the way life is these days. Guess back in her day, too."

He winced at these words. To Sandy, this all seemed as natural as baseball games and apple pie, even if she should be concerned about the consequences of immorality as the mother of two daughters. "If she did, do you realize that makes our father illegitimate?"

"Really, Neil. That's disgusting. You shouldn't be saying such things, especially since you never knew Dad. I was three when he died, and I remember him in his uniform and everything. He died fighting for his country. The least you can do is honor his memory. He doesn't deserve to be slapped with a label, especially over something that isn't his fault."

"I'm not doing anything of the sort. I am honoring his memory by finding out the truth for the sake of our family."

"Sometimes the truth is better left unsaid. I don't want you spoiling Christmas by bringing this up. We're all going to be together, and we're going to have a good time. So please, for all our sakes, let it go."

That was the proverbial saying of the night. *Let it go.* And just how was he supposed to do that? Life had been turned upside down in an instant. And now he was facing it head on.

Neil slept little that night, spending hours on his computer, scouring the Internet, and trying to find out more information about the family genealogy. He ran into brick walls on every turn. Without details and specifics, such as the phantom grandfather's name, he had little hope of discovering the truth.

During his time away from White Pines in his pursuit of the truth, he called the nursing unit to check on Gram. He had the nurses tell her he was under the weather, an understatement, to say the least. He never felt worse. All the respect he held for Gram, all the love he had for her, was now being put to the test. What if she did have a child out of wedlock, who happened to be his father? People do make mistakes. But Gram's swooning over his dad's father, when the man's memory should have been put away long ago, made Neil angry. If anything, such sin should be a closed book, not thrust wide open for all eyes to see.

When three days had passed, Neil realized he would have to venture back to White Pines and face the situation head-on. He didn't relish the encounter. The joy of spending that special time with Gram was lost on the heels of all this. It would be difficult concealing his feelings about it, too. Gram would sense something was up. She was far from senile but, rather, was as sharp as a tack. She'd know — which maybe was for the better. Maybe he could put this to rest, once and for all.

Arriving at White Pines, Neil decided to get his act together before he ventured up to Gram's room. He headed for the cafeteria and a cup of coffee, hoping he could come up with a way to salvage his relationship with Gram while finding out information at the same time. Hunkered down at the table, he was nursing his dilemma over a cup of hot brew laced with cream and sugar when he heard a friendly hello. He looked up to see Debbie standing over him, holding her own cup of coffee. He never thought the vision of a sweet and friendly face would stir him as much as her face did at that moment.

"Everything all right?"

He shrugged and took a swallow of coffee.

"I wanted to call, but you made it pretty clear that I should avoid you. So I did."

"That was a big mistake on my part."

She raised an eyebrow.

"I thought the two of us got my grandmother on some kind of strange track that made no sense. Now, after talking to my family, I think there may be something to her story."

"About your grandfather?"

"How he may not be the man I thought. My dad's father is not Grandpa Joe but a man I know nothing about."

Debbie sat down, her mouth a perfect O.

He nodded. "Mom acted pretty strange when I asked about it. My sister laughed it off, like the idea of Gram shacking up and having a child out of wedlock is no big deal. But it is to me. If I find out it's true, that we're all illegitimate, do you realize what kind of a stigma that is to live with?"

"Neil, if your grandmother did something in her past, it's like every other sin in our lives. God can erase it, as far as the east is from the west. He can make something good come out of it. And I think He already has. Look at you."

Neil wanted to accept the compliment she offered. Instead, he found himself sagging under the weight of it. To him, this sin left a stain that could not be erased. It would always be a part of him, this bloodline that was not Grandpa Joe's but some stranger's. "I have to find out from Gram who this man is, but I don't know how to go about asking. My family told me to forget about it.

But I can't."

"Neil, if it will help, I'll gladly ask Elvina about it. I can talk pretty openly with the residents. I'll try to discover what's going on so you won't be caught in the middle."

"That might be better. The truth is, I don't feel comfortable asking Gram about her past. I feel like a busybody. But, maybe, if you were to do a little probing . . ."

"Sure. As it is, Elvina's been pretty depressed since you stopped visiting. She won't eat her dinner. So you need to get up there on the double and assume your post." Debbie shot him a grin before looking at her watch. "Dinner is being served as we speak."

"So she isn't eating, huh?" He drained his coffee. "I can't have that happening. I'd better make tracks. And, Debbie . . . thanks a lot. You're a godsend."

Her smile warmed his heart and set him at ease. Despite the situation he now found himself in, he thanked God for leading Debbie across his path.

CHAPTER 7

Debbie mulled over everything as she drove to work the following morning. How does one handle a delicate matter like this, one so fragile that the situation could break apart if she wasn't careful? She didn't have the slightest idea. This was a tough walk, like trying to walk on pavement made of glass. Not only must she consider Elvina's feelings but Neil's, too. She liked the man a great deal and spent a good amount of time thinking about what had happened and the stress he must be enduring. She wasn't immune to stress herself, by any means, and couldn't help feeling sorry for his situation. Now he was depending on her to be a clever gumshoe in his time of need. She sighed, a bit fearful, and hoped she wouldn't let Neil down. Maybe if she succeeded, they would also succeed in their relationship, which appeared about ready to blossom. Maybe if they could handle this crisis successfully, they truly would be inseparable.

Debbie drove down the main road of Fincastle and spied a small antique store with windows decked out in holiday trim. A thought came to her. Parking in front of the establishment, she wandered inside. To her delight, she stumbled upon a box of old records, some from an era that Elvina was certain to enjoy on her old-fashioned record player. She went ahead and purchased the entire box. Maybe it would pave the way to a closer kinship with Elvina and perhaps an open door to her past.

Arriving at work, Debbie groaned when she saw Trish there. It had been peaceful the last few days on the floor with Trish taking some time off. Even Harold was calmer and not shouting down the menacing Germans like he usually did. It was as if the residents were more relaxed without Trish around.

"What is that?" Trish inquired, pointing to the phonograph records in Debbie's possession. "You never give up, do you? You still want to be the belle of the floor."

"I care about the residents."

"Ha. You mean you want them singing your praises so it makes the rest of us look bad." She glanced over at Natasha who nodded.

"Trish, I don't know why you're so concerned about what I'm doing. It would be nice if we all just worried about our own lives."

Mrs. Whitaker ducked into the nurses' lounge, telling them it was time to get their assignments. When she saw Debbie's armful of record albums, she asked about them.

"They're for Elvina," Debbie said proudly.

"What a wonderful idea. Maybe it will lift her mood a little. Since her grandson stopped visiting regularly, she hasn't been acting quite right. I think this is a great idea."

Debbie could nearly see the fire and brimstone spurting out of Trish's nostrils. As she went about her day, she sensed Trish glaring at her and whispering to the other nurses. Then things began to happen. Debbie's linen cart mysteriously disappeared. All the call lights for her patients came on at once. When she answered them, only to find nothing amiss, they were turned on again. She began to fume. If things weren't difficult enough, now she had to deal with coworkers acting like grade school kids.

When Trish and company left for lunch, Debbie used the time to present her gift to Elvina. She found the older woman sitting in her chair positioned in front of the window, though Debbie knew she couldn't see the pretty view of the evergreen trees. Love welled up within her at the sight of the woman, especially with the knowledge that this was Neil's beloved grandmother. "Hi, Elvina."

She turned her head and smiled. "Debbie, how are you?"

"I'm doing well."

"Why don't I have you today? I have that one who always sounds like she has a cold."

"I wish I had control over the assignments, Elvina, but it's the head nurse who makes them out." Debbie took a seat beside her. "I have something for you." Gently she placed a record on Elvina's lap.

"What is this?" She sniffed it. "Smells old. A record?"

"Yes. I found several of them in an antique store, and I thought you might like to hear some new tunes. There's one that has a song about a woodpecker, of all things."

Elvina began to glow. "How wonderful. I would love to hear it. I could use some laughter right about now."

Debbie obliged by starting up the player and putting on an album. Soon the room filled with the crazy tune. In no time, they were singing away with the lyrics and mimicking the song's funny woodpecker noises.

They both broke out in laughter at the song's conclusion. "Could your husband sing?" Debbie asked.

"Joe? Dear me, no. He couldn't carry a tune in a bucket, poor thing. He once told me how he tried out for the choir. The choirmaster thought he should do other things. He was very good at building. He made me a wonderful cabinet to store all my fine china. I certainly hope my daughter is taking good care of it."

Debbie began to fidget, wondering how she should broach the subject of the other man Elvina had talked to Neil about. "I think the oldies are still goodies."

"Oh, they certainly are. Now my Samuel, he had a wonderful singing voice. He would make me swoon with his voice. I told him he should go to Hollywood and star in a musical."

Debbie caught her breath. It seemed almost too good to be true. Elvina was actually talking about *him!* "I don't think I've heard about Samuel. Was he one of your sons?"

Elvina laughed long and loud. "Oh, you are a funny thing. Certainly not, though I often thought of naming one of my sons after him. I don't think Joe would have approved. He knew how close Samuel and I once were. I think Joe was afraid the man would show up on my doorstep one day, ready to whisk me away or something."

Even as Elvina spoke, Debbie began to rationalize all this out. Elvina must have once had two boyfriends competing for her love. Maybe they had tried to woo her in different ways, one with flowers and song, and the other with trips to the store for an ice cream float. Debbie had to admit she wouldn't mind two men fighting over her. There was a certain romantic lure to it all. Two men, each one interested, each one thinking she was special, each one wanting to share their life and love forever. Then she chastised herself. What was wrong with one special man wooing her with hot chocolate and a great smile? Neil was more than enough, in her opinion, and she hoped the feeling was mutual.

"I don't know what happened to him." Her voice softened. "For all I know, Samuel died on the battlefield."

Battlefield? Now Debbie was all ears.

"Maybe he never came back. Or if he came back, he never tried to contact me. Maybe even now he's wondering what happened to his Albert. But I did what he

113

wanted. I took care of his little boy while he was gone. I treated him as if he were my own."

"Hello! Excuse me! If this isn't much of a bother, your people are ringing their call lights, Debbie. And Harriet is nearly on the floor."

Debbie whirled to see Trish standing in the doorway, her arms folded. She stood up and followed Trish to the solarium to find one of the residents, the elderly Harriet Watson, leaning a bit sideways out of her chair. "Anyone could have helped her," Debbie grumbled, helping the woman sit upright with pillows at her sides to support her.

"We have enough to do without looking after your residents while you sing some dumb woodpecker song and hold Elvina's hand," Trish said in a huff.

Debbie burned with anger. Everything took flight, even the bit of joy over the way Elvina was beginning to open up about her past. Debbie soon began snapping at the residents. When one accidentally tipped over his tray of food, spilling it on the floor and leaving colorful patterns on her smock, she scolded him.

"Debbie, may I see you for a minute?"

Mrs. Whitaker spoke from the doorway of her office. Heat flooded Debbie's face at the thought of the head nurse witnessing her outbursts.

"Is everything all right?" asked Mrs. Whitaker. "I've never seen you lose your temper with the residents."

"I'm fine."

"Sometimes it can get very stressful around the holidays. The residents get more demanding."

"The personnel aren't much better."

Mrs. Whitaker raised her eyebrow.

"I'll be frank, Mrs. Whitaker. Trish and I do not get along at all."

"It's not like I haven't noticed. But we must do what we can in order to give the residents the best care possible. They are our priority."

"Trish doesn't think so. More than once, I've had to clean up after her. She doesn't brush their teeth. She never combs their hair. And she gets the praise of everyone on the floor just because she has the biggest mouth."

Mrs. Whitaker stood silent and still, studying her. Debbie knew she had blown it big-time. She'd let her irritation get the best of her. Though she wanted Mrs. Whitaker to know about Trish's work habits, she never expected it to come out this way. But maybe it was just as well. The truth had finally been let out of the bag instead of being hidden away for far too long.

"I will follow Trish and see what's happening. But I suggest, Debbie, that you concentrate on what you're doing. I can say that, after what I observed today, you are no different than Trish. Raising your voice with the residents is not proper care either."

"I know. I shouldn't have done it. I wasn't mad at them but at other things. And I took it out on them, which I shouldn't have."

"Debbie, I know we all experience frustrations here. I have my moments, too. But we have to be doubly careful to keep ourselves under control at all times." She nodded before returning to the computer screen to complete the day's charting.

Debbie shuffled out of the office, only to see Trish standing at the nurses' station, a funny grin painted on her face. If only she had an ally on this floor, someone who would vouch for her and what she had witnessed concerning Trish. But there was no one. No one cared. She was on her own. Talk about being on the battlefield of the enemy, alone, just like Harold warned. She was living it.

The work shift had ended by the time Debbie ventured back to see Elvina. She made certain that Trish and her cohorts had left before she returned to the room. Elvina was listening to one of the records she had brought. "I'm back, Elvina."

"I was thinking of you and wondered where you went."

"I had to take care of some residents." She shrugged. "It's just like one of the other residents said — I'm here on a battlefield without a friend in the world."

"Now, now." Elvina reached out her hand, which Debbie took. The older lady squeezed it. "You're my friend."

"Thanks, Elvina."

"In fact, I do believe you're my best friend. I don't have friends here. I don't talk to anyone except the girl at the beauty parlor. And, of course, Nathaniel."

"Why don't you go play bingo or do some crafts?"

"I like the minister at the Sunday services. But I think people see me and decide they can't talk to me because I'm blind and can't see them. Or maybe I make them uncomfortable, and they think they will say the wrong words."

"It must be hard."

"I was thankful to see what I could before the glaucoma took away my sight. I saw my dear husband and my children."

"And you saw Samuel, too."

"Samuel! I told you about Samuel? My goodness, I haven't told anyone about Samuel. I saw him before he left to go to war. World War II, you know. And he told me . . ." She paused.

All at once, Debbie saw her gray blue eyes fill with tears. Elvina's hand fell away to rest in her lap, which was covered by a knitted lap robe.

"He asked me to take care of his little boy. He had a boy, you know. The little boy's mother died in childbirth. That's what Samuel told me. And he asked me to look after his Albert while he was gone to war. And I did, Debbie, even when Samuel didn't come home. Little Albert became part of our family when I married Joe. He grew up and married Terrie. And they had three children: Richard, Sandra, and Nathaniel J. But Albert died so young, the poor thing. He died in Vietnam."

Debbie stared in disbelief. Despite the sadness of it all, the truth rang loud and clear. Neil indeed had another grandfather, a man he never knew, a man who went off to war and left his father in Elvina's care. "And you have no idea what happened to Samuel?"

She shook her head. "I heard from him once. I used to have the letter. I don't know whatever happened to it. I should have put it in a frame. It's gone now, as are most of my things. But I can remember it clearly, as if he had written it yesterday. He told me how rainy and cold it was in England. He said they would soon go and free France. He said there wasn't anything better than fighting to free others. He told me to give Albert a hug and tell him his father loved him."

Tears trickled down her plump cheeks. Debbie leaned over and plucked two tissues out of the box, one for Elvina and one for herself.

"I read the letter to Albert. He was only three. He took it in his hands and held it to his heart. What a sweet sight. It was the closest he ever came to his father since he left for war, the handwriting on that paper. I would show the letter to him every so often, telling him his father wrote it after he went off to war. When he was about ten, he asked about the war. I told him as best I could. But I didn't want to share how I used to feel about Samuel, since I was married to Joe, you know. Those things shouldn't come out. I loved my Joe." She blew her nose. "And yes, I loved Samuel, too. But it was different. A different kind of love. In a different time and place. And that time is gone.

119

But I wish it would come back. I wish I could know where he is. I wish I could see him one last time, show him his grandchildren. He would be so proud. But it's a Christmas gift well beyond anyone's ability to give."

Debbie left White Pines, her thoughts fairly spinning over this emotional revelation. It seemed too unbelievable to be real, yet it was. And she was in on it all, along with Neil. *Neil.* She would have to tell Neil the truth. What would he think? How would he react? Would the news push them away or bring them closer? She didn't know as she hugged her arms around her to ward off the chilly December night. She would have to tell him and let God handle the rest.

CHAPTER 8

Neil felt like Watson meeting Sherlock, only Debbie didn't appear for this meeting dressed in a full-length trench coat. Instead, she sat opposite him in the coffee shop in a fuzzy blue sweater. A shaggy scarf dangled around her neck, and she wore gold hoop earrings. She looked radiant. When she called earlier to invite him for coffee, he nearly fell over. A woman hadn't invited him to do anything in ages. He took the coffee-and-bagel invite as the next best thing to dinner at a five-star restaurant. Of course this was hardly some special date. From the seriousness of her expression as she sipped her cappuccino, this was strictly business. But he hoped more might come out of the conversation in the end.

"You were right, Neil," she began.

I was right? That was news to him. So far, it seemed he hadn't been right about anything. After the fiasco at his mother's, the phone call to his sister, and a fruitless Internet search to try and hunt down clues to his past, he only saw doors slamming in every direction.

"You have a different grandfather on your dad's side."

The coffee caught in his throat. He coughed, quickly covering his mouth with a napkin before he made a fool out of himself by splattering coffee down the front of his sweater.

"Are you all right? I can hit you on the back or something, but if you're coughing, that usually means you're okay."

"I'm okay," he said in a raspy voice. "I should have swallowed first before you broke the news. How did you find out?"

"Elvina told me. Took awhile, but she finally did. His name was Samuel."

"Samuel what?"

Debbie's full red lips turned pouty. For some reason, she looked absolutely kissable at that moment, and he couldn't figure out why. She had just dropped a bombshell of some unknown grandfather. Kissing should be the furthest activity from his mind. Maybe he should simply ditch all this soap opera stuff — the strange grandfather, his family's weird reactions, Gram's longing to see some old flame — and enjoy this budding relationship. That would be nice. Maybe soon. First he had to get this resolved.

"She never mentioned his last name. All I know is, he went off to war."

"Which war? We've had plenty."

"The Civil War."

A twinkle in her eye now accompanied her upturned lips. If not for the table separating them at this moment and the seriousness of this discussion, he might be forced to act on his impulses and skip to the kissing part. "Very funny. We've had several wars in the twentieth century. World War I and II. Korean War, Vietnam. Desert Storm. Afghanistan. Iraq. Of course I'm pretty sure it wasn't any of the later ones."

"World War II. He left his boy behind, Elvina said, asking that she take care of him while he was away. The little boy's mother had died giving birth, it seems. How sad. And the boy's name was Albert."

Again his throat tickled, but at least he wasn't in the midst of swallowing coffee. He coughed. "That was my dad's name. Albert Jenson."

"He must've had a different last name, though, before he was adopted into the Jenson family. Maybe you can ask your mom what it was."

He shuddered at the thought of another confrontation with his mother. "I don't think I can. She wasn't too keen about me prying into this matter in the first place. All she and Sandy told me to do was let it go. But I think I have the right to know who my true grandparents are. There's nothing wrong about wanting to know one's heritage."

"Or knowing, for instance, if you're predisposed to hereditary traits," Debbie added. "I mean, when you fill out physicals, you have to give a family history of illnesses, such as heart disease, cancer, or some other diseases in the family."

He began turning his cup. A bit of coffee spotted the table, probably from the first coughing episode, and now it made a perfect brown ring. "Did Gram say what happened to Samuel?"

"No, and that's where the real mystery comes in. She said she never received word about his circumstances. Once he shipped out overseas, she got one letter from him, and that was all. I think it's strange that a man who left behind a son he obviously loved would suddenly disappear. My thinking is, he probably went missing in action."

"Maybe. Then why would Gram want to see him again?"

"I suppose she wants to know what happened — to close that chapter in her life. She has little else to think about in her wheelchair all day, you know. You get to thinking about the past. And obviously she has been thinking about Samuel."

Neil sighed. He wished there were more to go on. Like a last name for the man. What unit he was with. He might have been able to do some further research on the Internet. It might take another trip home, maybe when his mother was preoccupied with her quilting bee. He had a key to the house. He could go over there and do some hunting to avoid further family turmoil over this. Though he wished his mother would just come out and tell him what she knew and save him the trouble of digging for answers. Obviously the idea of some other man in the family line raised questions some would rather leave unasked. But it was important to him. His bloodline was not of the true Jenson. He was not a true relation to Gram — or to any of those relatives on his dad's side he saw at holidays or at reunions. He had no true grandmother, paternal aunts, uncles, or even cousins, as far as he knew.

He sucked in his breath. Is this how his father once felt? Did he, too, wonder who his real parents were? If he had any other siblings? Or did he just accept Gram, Grandpa Joe, and those who loved him, casting away the mystery concerning the identity of his real parents. If only Neil could ask him. If only he knew his own dad, too. Now he had two lost loved ones, his grandfather and his dad, who didn't know that he, Neil, lived and breathed, that he carried on their characteristics, that he was alive and doing pretty good for himself, all things considered.

"Neil?" Debbie asked, staring at him with a questioningly look in her deep blue eyes. Against the fuzzy blue sweater, those eyes looked even more intense. "Are you okay?"

"Oh sure."

"I'm not so sure. You look like one of the Lost Boys in Never-Never Land. You haven't said anything."

"Maybe I am a lost boy. I don't know who I am, at least half of me, that is. I don't know my grandparents on my dad's side. I don't know my relatives. Not even my father. I feel like a half-baked orphan. I never would have believed it until just a few days ago. Then some deep, dark secret pops out when you least expect it. Now I have to deal with it. To be honest, I don't know if I want to."

"It has to be hard. But you realize there

are people who love you even if you don't have a direct bloodline to them. Like Elvina. Despite everything, you're her grandson, through and through. And that's what counts — the love you've had for each other all your lives. You need to look at it that way, Neil."

He chuckled. "We're sure good for each other, Debbie, telling each other how to have a positive outlook. I would almost venture to say we were made for each other."

He saw her inhale swiftly. A red tide flooded her cheeks. She stared down at her cappuccino. Nothing came out for several moments. The seconds of solitude were agonizing. "What I meant is, we seem to have the right words to say to each other when the going gets rough," he added hastily.

"I guess we do."

The conversation became stilted after that. A short time later, they were saying good-bye and going their separate ways. Neil sighed in disappointment. He shouldn't have brought the conversation to such a personal level. He didn't need to thrust all his problems on her, even if he did feel an unmistakable attraction for her. Though he did agree with his assessment that they were made for each other. They helped each other when life dealt out one trial after another. They stood together, supporting one another. And God showed He cared, through an attractive woman named Debbie.

Neil spent the rest of the day idle, paying little attention to the insurance claims mounting on his desk at work. Instead, he gazed at the table and a miniature twinkling Christmas tree that one of the secretaries had placed there. He considered his past, present, and future, even though he had made light of it when Debbie first asked him. The past had now reared its head; even when he wanted to leave it alone, God had seen fit to resurrect it. Maybe he needed to deal with it — not only the other grandfather issue, but the idea of not having a dad and losing out on that part of his life. Until now, he hadn't realized that, perhaps, there were things he needed to resolve in his heart, a deep aching, a hole that a dad never did fill. Sure, Mom had brought his uncles around for the influence of men in his life. But as he'd recently learned, they weren't even his true relatives on his dad's side. They weren't truly his family. And it made him feel strange.

Later that evening, Neil headed to his mom's house. It sat dark and silent but for the white lights left burning on a few outside bushes. Using the key to open the kitchen door, he ventured inside. Immediately he inhaled the delicious aroma of dinner earlier that night. *Meat loaf.* Raiding the refrigerator to make a meat loaf sandwich, he then headed to the basement and Mom's place for storing everything under the sun. He was looking for a clue, something that would link him to this strange man who went off to fight at Normandy. Some name that could help him with an Internet search. Something tangible he could hold on to and not let go.

An hour later, he was still rummaging through boxes of old snapshots. There were a few of his father as a youth. He recognized Gram in many of them. Scribbled on the back, in his grandmother's stately handwriting, were the words: Al, 1950, ten years old. Al, 1952. Then he found one labeled Al, 1948. He was getting closer. His heart began to thump in anticipation.

Suddenly a door banged upstairs. *Oh no!* Was it time for his mother to be home already?

"Who's here?" her voice called out. "Sandy?"

Neil froze. He stuffed the pictures back in the box as footsteps sounded on the stairs.

"Just me, Mom."

"Neil?" His mother appeared as he sat guiltily on the floor, surrounded by photo boxes. "What on earth are you doing?"

"Gram confessed to a friend of mine, Mom. Grandpa Joe is not my true grandfather. His name was Samuel."

Her hand flew to her forehead. "I have a terrible headache, Neil. That's why I came home early. I can't take this right now."

"I'm sorry you don't feel good, Mom. But please, I just need a little information. Like Dad's real name before the Jenson family adopted him. That's all I need. Then I'll be out of your hair. Promise."

"Why do you insist on doing this, Neil?"

He stared, surprised she would ask him. "So I can find out about my true grandfather. Mom, this is important. It's like any adopted child who wants to know about their real parents. What if this man had some kind of family gene we don't know about? Like genes for cancer, heart disease, or a blood condition. Sandy and Dick should know, too. I can research the Internet for the family tree."

"Well, what harm is there? All right. His last name was Truett. T-R-U-E-T-T." She collapsed in a chair. "Your father told me about the man from what Elvina relayed to him as a youngster — that his father's name was Samuel Truett and that he went off to war. He fought in the Battle of Normandy. He wrote Al and Elvina once and then was never heard from again."

"Does anyone know what happened to him?"

"No one knows. Elvina always hung on to the hope that he was alive, maybe living somewhere in France. If that were the case, then why didn't he check on Al? We always believed he died in the war. But no one knows for certain. There was no record. I think he was even listed as missing in action, but I'm not sure."

"I know there was a lot of confusion at the Battle of Normandy, with GIs being in the wrong place and with the wrong units. He must've gotten lost in it all."

"Really, Neil, it was so long ago. I don't know why Elvina is bringing this up and dragging you into the middle of it. It just isn't right." She stood up and headed for the stairs. "I need some hot tea. But after tonight, I don't want to hear anything more about it."

Neil looked at the box of pictures at his feet. He felt bad, putting this kind of stress on his mom. Maybe he should let things go and let the past stay the past. But he couldn't shake the vision of Gram wanting to know what happened. And this was Dad's father. He had a desire to know. A right, even. And he hoped Mom would understand.

Neil wasn't certain what to say or do when he came to see Gram a few evenings later. He had called the facility to leave a message that he would not be in for several days. He spent that time hunkered down at his computer, doing every kind of a viable search for Samuel Truett. There were Web sites devoted to veterans of the Normandy invasions. He managed to find Samuel's unit and where they fought, but little else. There was not even conclusive evidence as to where he might have ended up, whether dead on the beach or somewhere in France. It was a bit of consolation, at least, to see the name of his actual grandfather there on the computer screen. He wished he knew what the man looked like. Looking in the mirror earlier that day as he readied himself for work, he wondered if he possessed any of the characteristics on his dad's side. Maybe the nose? The color of eyes? That persistent small tuft of hair that drooped down over his forehead?

He was glad to share all this with Debbie

over the phone that evening. He told her what he'd learned, about Samuel's full name and his place in history on D-day. As usual, she was her own confident self, claiming that God was about ready to blow wide open the doors on his past. He hoped so.

As he arrived at White Pines that evening, he prayed that Gram would be in the mood to talk about things. It all depended on her frame of mind.

In the parking lot, he saw a tall nurse with blond hair unlocking the door to her car. She looked up then. A smile easily formed with teeth that gleamed like pearls. "Hi, Neil."

I'm not in the mood for this. And I have a nurse I like very much, thank you. Try the next guy.

"I'm Trish, remember? You hired me to take care of your grandma over Christmas."

The comment stopped him in his tracks. With everything else going on, he had forgotten his idea to bring Gram home, and the plan for this Trish to care for her.

"Hey, listen. I have a few minutes. Wanna grab some coffee, and we can talk about her care?"

His fingers began to curl inside the pockets of his coat. "Actually I haven't yet arranged for it all. I'll have to let you know when things are settled." He wanted to ask if there was any way she might switch with Debbie and allow her to come, but before he could form his thoughts into words, Trish stepped forward.

"Hey, I was talking to Natasha, and she was telling me about this great movie that just came out. Some kind of funny Christmas comedy. A bunch of us nurses on the floor were thinking of going. Wanna come along with us?"

The invitation momentarily stunned him. "Is this some kind of floor event?"

"Yeah, we nurses like to get together sometimes and go to the movies. Kind of a tradition every year to see the season's latest Christmas flick. But since there aren't many guys working here, except in the cafeteria or in maintenance, we'd love to have you come along to give us some atmosphere. I mean, you're a regular on the floor. You practically live there, kind of." She giggled.

He chuckled in response. If this was a floor event, no doubt Debbie was also going. That idea appealed to him, considering how his life had been topsy-turvy recently. A few laughs with Debbie and her nursing buddies might be just the thing he needed. "Okay."

Trish's face lit up as if she had been plugged like a strand of Christmas lights into a socket. "Great!" Trish exclaimed. "We're going tomorrow night at seven. The Regal Theater in Roanoke. You can visit your grandma and then join us. It's going to be great."

He shuffled off, glad for some kind of outing with Debbie besides the coffee shop, even if it were with the other nurses on the floor. They had done little else but immerse themselves in this grandfather mystery. Maybe in the theater, he could sneak her away from the crowd to a seat on the opposite side. There they could indulge in a bucket of popcorn and conversation. For once, he had something to look forward to besides thinking about his family situation. And that made things easier to handle, at least for now.

CHAPTER 9

"Hey, Debbie, Neil here. Hope you're doing well. Looking forward to seeing you tonight. Should be a lot of fun. I'm planning to pick you up around six. See you then."

Huh? What is he talking about? Debbie heard the cryptic message loud and clear on the answering machine but couldn't quite believe it. She racked her brain, trying to remember if she had agreed to do something with Neil tonight. Had they made plans during the coffee outing a few days ago and she'd forgotten about it? Looking at the calendar, there was nothing written in. But they must've set up something for him to say what he did on the answering machine. As it was, ever since the encounter at the coffee shop, she found herself in a daze. Despite the conversation about Neil's grandfather, it wasn't like other past encounters. Something had changed in

136

Neil . . . an interest that had not been there before, as if their casual friendship had taken a personal turn. Of course Debbie would like nothing better, but it still made her feel jittery, like a girl on her first date. Was she ready for this new turn onto some unknown path with a man she had only recently begun to understand?

She decided to go along with whatever the preplanned engagement was, in the hopes that something might clue her in. Maybe this was Neil's way of leading her by the hand down that new path in their relationship. Staring at her wardrobe, she wondered what to wear for a mystery date, finally settling on a jean skirt and a Christmas sweater. That should work for almost anything.

When the doorbell rang, Debbie opened her door to find a cheerful and expectant Neil. *This must be a great time we set up,* she thought with a sigh. *If only I knew what.*

"Do you have any idea what movie you were going to see?" he asked as they stepped out into the blustery evening air. "I know where the theater is in Roanoke, but I haven't been by there in a while to see what's playing."

"Uh . . ." *Did I agree to see a movie?* "I'm not sure, Neil."

"So Trish didn't tell you, huh? I guess it doesn't matter."

Trish? What does she have to do with this? "No, she didn't. We don't talk much."

"Hmm. I know it's some kind of comedy. I think it has something to do with Christmas."

Debbie was growing more uncomfortable by the minute and more depressed at the thought of Neil and Trish conversing. Obviously Trish had invited him to see a movie. Then why was he dragging her along? To be a chaperone? To dump her somewhere when the timing was right and run off to be with Trish? *Really, Debbie, get a life. This guy is no Brad. He's a gentleman.* Besides, they had been getting along famously. He had shown an obvious interest at the coffee shop. Then why was Trish suddenly mixed up in all of this?

"You're awfully quiet," he observed.

How do I tell him nicely that I have no idea what is going on? "Neil, I have no idea what is going on." The statement popped out of her mouth like an exploding cork.

"What do you mean?"

"I mean, tonight. You leave me a message on the answering machine, but I don't recall us setting up any kind of special outing to a theater."

138

"You know — the annual movie gig you gals go to every Christmas. Trish told me all about it — how you nurses get together to see the latest Christmas movie playing. She decided since I was a regular on the floor, I could tag along."

I don't believe it. That woman is too much. "Neil, I'm sorry to say this, but I know nothing about our floor's staff attending a movie tonight. That's not to say they aren't going. Trish gets the other nurses together to do things, even has them over to her place. They go out to the mall in Roanoke and other places — a regular groupie thing. But I've never been invited to those events. I don't fit into their mold, I guess, which is probably for the best."

He looked as if he didn't believe her. "I assumed you were a part of this, being a floor thing. That's the main reason I said yes, thinking you'd be there."

At least that part proved gratifying and even endearing. "Look, I'll be honest with you. Trish and I don't get along at all. She really dislikes me, and I must say, the feeling is mutual, despite the fact I've tried not to make enemies."

He turned off at the nearest exit and came to a stop in the parking lot of a gas station. "I had no idea. Wow, I'm sorry. I shouldn't

139

have assumed all this. It was pretty dumb."

"It's okay. You can just take me home and go on to see the movie, whatever it is."

"So you still don't want to go? We can get our own seats. It'll be fun. We deserve it."

"I'm sorry, but sitting in the same theater with Trish would be the worst kind of agony. I know that sounds mean. I wish I could say that things were okay between us, but they aren't." Then it all came tumbling out — how Trish was considered the belle of White Pines, even though her work ethics left much to be desired. The way she treated the residents. How everyone loved Trish but left others like Debbie hanging out to dry. How Debbie wished she had the right words to say. Why people didn't notice her efforts but applauded Trish instead. "I just wish I could tell the head nurse, Mrs. Whitaker, about it all."

Neil sat there, still and silent, as if Debbie had delivered a major blow to his life. "I wish I had known about this earlier," he said glumly. "Now what am I supposed to do?"

"Sorry. I didn't mean to burst a bubble or something."

"I hired this Trish gal to take care of Gram for the holidays."

"You what?" Debbie nearly jumped in her seat. "Neil, you can't have her do that."

140

"No, I can't, not after what you've been telling me about the way she treats the residents. No wonder Gram always seems depressed whenever Trish takes care of her. I thought it was because of the holiday season or the memories of this other grandfather. How could I have been so stupid?"

Debbie saw the anger fill him. His fingers tightened around the steering wheel.

"I don't like being taken for a ride."

"Neil, you didn't know. You were trying to give your grandmother a nice Christmas. There's still time to find someone else."

He didn't seem to hear her. She sucked in her breath, watching the rigid lines forming on his face. "Hey, it's no big deal."

"I don't like someone pulling the wool over my eyes, and that's all I've been enduring these last few weeks. A wool coat thrown over my head. Maybe a whole coatrack. Between this whole grandfather scenario and some whacked-out dame pulling a few fast ones, I don't know what's going on. But I plan to set the record straight, once and for all."

Tires spit gravel as the car took off, making a fast U-turn and heading back toward Fincastle. Debbie had no idea what to say so she kept quiet until Neil drove into the lot of her apartment building. Debbie offered to brew him a cup of the peach tea he liked, hoping it might calm him down enough to think rationally. But the lines of irritation were clearly written on his face like lines drawn in the sand.

Moments later, she handed him the freshly brewed tea in the bear nursing mug. "Neil, all I ask is that you don't do something you and I will both regret. Especially me. I still work at that place, you know. You stir up the hornet's nest, and guess who will get stung."

"I understand, Debbie, but some things in life need to be said. And it's high time someone told it like it is and didn't beat around the bush. The fact is, this woman needs to respect and treat human beings with dignity and not like playthings for her amusement. And you said so yourself that you wanted people to know about it."

Debbie flushed. She could just imagine the reaction if he strode in there with his emotional guns fully loaded. *But he doesn't understand Trish, nor does he have any inkling where this all might lead. And it won't be Trish's head that rolls.* There were all sorts of scriptures that told how to treat one's enemy — such as turning the other cheek when someone strikes you, or heaping coals of fire on another's head by not reciprocating evil for evil but rather answering evil with good. She mentioned them. "So just tell her that the plans have changed, that you don't want her working for you. Please don't go to Mrs. Whitaker about it. Let it go at that."

He slapped his hand across his forehead. "Good grief, there it is again — 'Let it go.' The saying of the century." He laughed long and loud on a sarcastic note. "That's all I've been hearing. I should get a T-shirt made up with those words on the front: LET IT GO. Let your grandfather go, Neil. Let everything go and allow the chips to fall where they may. Let people lie to you. Let the past sneak up on you. Forget that you have another grandfather or that some women will do anything to sucker you in." He threw the tea down his throat. "Guess what? I won't let it go. Not when there's a manipulative woman out there trying to take advantage of the elderly and others. These things need to be straightened out. If we let people do whatever they want, how is justice served?"

"If you must be the judge, at least be tactful. Don't storm in there and nail her to the wall. It will only backfire. There are ways to be wise as a serpent but gentle as a dove."

But the way Neil was looking at the moment, being tactful and acting like some dove were the furthest thoughts from his mind. And no amount of warm peach tea was going to stem the tide either. She sighed. There was nothing she could do. She was witnessing Neil's raw side. Better it came out now, she supposed. She wanted to find out more about him, didn't she? And now she was, even though she wondered where it might lead in the end.

Something definitely had changed when Debbie walked onto the floor a few days later. It began with her floating to another unit instead of staying on her normal floor. She disliked being away from the residents she had come to cherish. And her reassignment wasn't just for one day. Every day, she showed up to work on her own unit, and every day, Mrs. Whitaker sent her elsewhere. In the corner of the nursing lounge, she could see Trish sitting there with a wry smile, chattering with her friends. Debbie couldn't help but wonder what was going on. She didn't want to think Neil had anything to do with this. What had he said about the whole scenario that led to this change? Had he arranged to have her moved from the floor to keep her and Trish apart?

Debbie tried to involve herself in her

work, but she felt like she was walking on a sheet of ice, slipping and sliding, ready for another bruising. All the joy she had found in her work had vanished. At the noon hour, she went back to the floor and asked to see Mrs. Whitaker. The head nurse seemed preoccupied when she arrived, shuffling papers, looking at her watch, appearing as if she would rather be anywhere else than in a meeting with her. Or was it simply Debbie's imagination?

"I don't understand why I've been assigned to float, Mrs. Whitaker," Debbie started, taking a seat in the office. "I haven't been on this unit all week."

She sighed. "Debbie, it's my duty to send extra nurses on staff to where the need is the greatest."

"But no one else is floating. Just me."

Her face became rigid. "I have it in confidence that several people have witnessed some rather shocking things from you recently with regard to the residents and staff here on this floor. And I've even had some complaints from the residents."

She sat there, stunned. "What? But I haven't done anything."

"There have been complaints of you being short with the residents. I've seen it myself. You've let your assigned residents fall out of their wheelchairs. Trish even said she had to help because you weren't there. We can't have residents falling on the floor, breaking bones."

Debbie fumed, remembering but a single such incident, when she had been singing a song with Elvina and Trish informed her of a resident sliding out of her chair. But Trish had placed far more residents in harm's way in one week's time than Debbie had in her eight years of working here. "Trish isn't telling the truth. . . ."

"It isn't just Trish, but just about everyone on the unit who is complaining. I'm sorry, Debbie, but I think it's best if you float for now until I have you transferred to another floor. I know how you told me that you and Trish don't get along. So I think it's for the best if the two of you work on different units."

Trish and her gang are at it again, and this time at full throttle. Anger welled within her. Debbie felt her cheeks heat to a high intensity. "Trish should be the one transferred instead of me. I've done nothing wrong."

"Debbie, I've made up my mind. Trish has been here longer than you anyway. So we will look to having you transferred as soon as there's an opening. If you will excuse me, I have some paperwork to do."

Debbie felt as though she were living out her worst nightmare. The fog of life grew even thicker as she stumbled out of the office. How could this be happening? She knew why it happened. Neil must have made everyone irate, and now Trish had gathered the troops to have her permanently removed from the floor. Debbie had enemies worse than the Germans who plagued Harold's waking state, and her enemies worked right here with her. They had succeeded in taking her away from the residents she loved with all her heart.

Debbie went into the bathroom, locked the door, and sat down on the floor. Great heaves rose up in her throat. The injustice, the pain, was overwhelming. Is this what it felt like to be condemned without cause? To be punished for doing nothing but caring for others? *Is this what it's like, Jesus? I can't stand it. It hurts. I hurt.* She began to choke, almost as if she needed to vomit up the injustice. Slowly standing up, she gazed at her reflection in the mirror. Her eyes were red. Her brown hair hung in disarray. She looked as defeated as she felt.

Debbie could hardly wait for the shift to be over. Before she left, she decided to go and see Harold. She felt a kinship with him now that a real-life enemy had come to do battle. Harold would understand, somehow. When she arrived, he didn't look much better than she felt. He sat in his chair, leaning over to one side, his chin sunk into his hand, his bloodshot eyes staring blankly. Likely he was seeing images of the war again. Little did he know there was a fierce war going on right now. A spiritual war. A war of good and evil.

"Hi, Harold."

His head lifted. "It's you! Where have you been? I've been looking for you everywhere."

"I've been battling an enemy," she said glumly.

He gripped the armrests of his wheelchair as if the words brought him to life. "You've seen the enemy? Report your findings to the major. We need an accurate report of their movements."

For some reason, his words imparted comfort. He didn't know what had happened to her, but his propensity for war and battle seemed appropriate for the occasion. "There are enemies right here on this floor, you know."

"I know that. I've seen them. They pretend to wear white, but they are wolves in sheep's clothing."

She stared in wonder and amazement at

the scriptural quote that proved quite apropos to her situation. For a man supposedly not in tune with reality, Harold knew his Bible. And he knew what was happening all around him. "You are so right, Harold."

"I know them. Spies, they are. They work for the enemy. You have to be careful of them because they are here among our troops. Walk carefully. Keep alert."

"Yes, they're sneaking around, telling lies. And the lies seem to be working. They are having too much influence on the higher-ups." *Way too much,* she thought glumly.

He took her hand and gripped it. "It may seem that way, but, my dear girl, you should never give up. Don't think for a minute that they've won."

"That's all easier said than done. If only I knew what to do."

"Just keep quiet for now. Lay low. Wait. And when the moment comes, you can expose them for who they are."

She had to smile until the reality of her situation sobered her. "I won't have the time to expose their deeds. I'm being transferred."

"You're being transferred?"

"The boss thought it was for the best. I won't be a part of this unit anymore."

Harold shook his head. "You can't do that.

Not now. It's the enemy playing tricks. You have to watch them. They are crafty. But don't you go. Tell the major you need to be here. Tell him you need to finish your mission. If you go, others are gonna die. You have to accomplish your mission."

She stared in wonder at the frail man sitting there in his wheelchair. Harold spoke more like a messenger from God than Debbie could have imagined. If only she could believe it and not think of him as lost in another time and place. "Thanks, Harold."

He smiled and sat back as if his own mission were accomplished. But to Debbie, it looked like her mission had folded under the attack of the enemy. The mere thought depressed her greatly.

Heading for the car that afternoon, she decided this spelled the end. She would give her resignation at the end of the pay cycle and be done with all this misery.

CHAPTER 10

Once inside the safety of her apartment, Debbie chose not to turn on the lights. Instead, she put on the night-light above the stove and sat in the tiny living room in the dark. The dismal surroundings mirrored her soul at the moment, shadowed by a dark thundercloud. Angry tears smarted her eyes. She hoped she could disappear from this area and never be heard from again. Dad knew northern Virginia like the back of his hand. She would go back to her roots and look for a job there. Start fresh. Her parents would be happy to have her home. They would provide all the help she needed in finding a job and another place to live. She could search out old friends from high school, people she'd abandoned to come here. She missed good friends. It would be a safe refuge and a great escape. She would leave the whole mess behind her — Trish and her gang, Mrs. Whitaker's accusations, everything, and start over. Just so long as none of it followed after her.

Debbie went into the kitchen, turned on a light, and began taking down dishes to start the packing process. The nursing mugs promptly went into the garbage. Time to move on with her life. Leave here and never look back. Pretend White Pines, Elvina, Harold, and, yes, Neil never happened. She paused.

Neil.

She picked out the mug from the garbage she had used to serve him tea. Staring at it, her eyes welled with tears before she put the mug back in the trash can. She had no choice. This was the best way.

At that moment, the doorbell rang. Debbie contemplated ignoring it. Instead, she crept over to the door and peeked through the security hole.

Oh no! It's him.

"Debbie? You in there?"

Yes, and I'm perfectly miserable. You wanted to take revenge, and I end up the casualty, just like I thought I would. Wounded and about ready to run.

"Debbie, I saw your car parked in front of your place, so I know you're in there."

She chewed on her lip. "What do you want?"

152

"I heard what happened. Gram told me. She heard you were being transferred. Let me in, okay?"

"Just leave me alone."

"Debbie, please. I'm here to say I'm sorry."

She leaned closer to the door, intrigued by the concern radiating in his voice.

"This is my fault entirely. Please let me in."

In an instant, she opened the door. He stood dressed in his thick wool coat, staring at her, his eyes hollow. "You lose electricity or something?"

Debbie turned on a light in the living room. "I like it dark. Fits my mood."

Slowly he shed his coat and sat down on the sofa. "I know what's been happening to you, and I blame myself entirely. Gram told me you haven't been on the unit all week. She said you were working on other floors. A nurse told her."

"Big deal."

"I know you cautioned me to use tact when confronting Trish. I'll admit I didn't, and I have a feeling this is revenge."

"I don't know what was said, but somehow those people are painting me out to be the villain — telling the head nurse the things that Trish has done wrong and blaming them on me. None of it is true either. I don't know what to do." She slumped down, resting her chin in her hand.

"Then I'll make sure that woman is locked up with the key thrown away." Neil stood up and began to pace.

"Neil, it's that kind of attitude that got me into this mess in the first place."

He whirled around.

"I asked you to please use tact. I don't know what you said, but it really backfired. Now everyone hates me."

He sighed. "I guess displaying tact was the furthest thing from my mind. I really laid into Trish. I told her flat out that she isn't going to work with my grandmother or anyone else until she gets her act together. And I warned her to leave you alone. Obviously my threats didn't accomplish what I intended."

"No, they didn't."

"You warned me. I guess I let my anger get the best of me."

"Trish hired her cronies to back up her story about me being a wretched aide. And the head nurse, Mrs. Whitaker, is buying it all. She's going to fork over my transfer even before the ink on the paper is dry. But I don't plan on giving her — or anyone there — the satisfaction of watching me being run off the floor."

Neil stiffened. His hand reached out to her. "Debbie, I'm really sorry this happened. I'll talk to the head nurse myself and straighten this out."

"No, thanks." She stood up. "As far as I'm concerned, this is my signal to move back to my hometown. I'm giving my resignation in a week and leaving this place." She returned to the kitchen to take pots out of the cupboard. "Even if things do get straightened out, there'll still be tension on the unit. I think it's best for all our sakes if I make tracks and leave. It's almost the end of the month. I can get out of my rental agreement easier then, too."

"What? Are you crazy?"

"Everyone else thinks I am. I can make a break. Dad has been asking me to move back to northern Virginia anyway. There are plenty of jobs around there. Maybe I can even finish my education and become an RN."

His face turned pasty white as he looked at the dishes mounting on the table. "Debbie, please don't do this."

"It's better this way. For everyone."

He stared in disbelief. "So, because of my stupidity, you're going to jump ship?" He snapped his fingers. "I never pegged you for a quitter, even if things got a little rough. This can be fixed, you know. I will do whatever it takes."

Her anger escalated within. "I'm not quitting. I'm moving on to bigger and better things. You try working in a place like that. Nurses ganging up on you. Residents who don't care what you do for them. Never getting any thanks but a slap in the face, and for something you didn't even do. Then you went and told everyone off when I pleaded with you not to. You took matters into your own hands, as though my opinion didn't count. And now I end up being the one who gets burned."

His cheeks turned from white to crimson red. "So you've made up your mind, and nothing I can say is going to change it."

"That's about right."

He went to the living room and gathered up his coat. "Look, I know I blew it. I'm willing to fix this. But if all you want to do is bolt, then it makes no sense for me to do anything, does it?"

He stood for a few lingering moments, no doubt hoping she would change her mind. When she didn't answer, he turned and left. As soon as the door shut behind him, Debbie looked back at the dishes. She went to the trash can and again took out the nursing mug in which she had served Neil the tea. Fingering the bear dressed in a nursing uniform, she promptly broke into tears.

What can I do, God? I made this mess, and now Debbie is moving away because of it. Help me figure this out.

The dilemma plagued him all night. Another sleepless night. Another night of contemplation, and this time it did not concern his grandfather. He was about to see the one woman who stirred him like no other leave the area, never to be heard from again. The woman with whom he was falling head over heels in love was now a casualty. To lose Debbie would be like losing a part of himself. They were alike in so many ways. They thought alike. They both loved God. But, if Debbie had already made up her mind to leave, there was little he could do. He could try to remedy the situation at her workplace, yes. Pray, yes. But the decision to stay or go was hers alone. He only wished she would consider him in the equation. Maybe she had no deep feelings for him. Maybe he was just a buddy, a brother, a temporary friend until the going got rough. There was no meaningful relationship to keep her here, and that's why she felt she could leave.

Neil decided he must try to fix this, even if Debbie was determined to leave. He had not followed her advice. He had approached Trish with his anger evident, telling her he wouldn't hire her if she were the last nurse available, ordering her to show some respect for the residents instead of treating them as objects for her amusement. Debbie had asked him to be tactful, but tactful he was not. Debbie's bit of wisdom might have saved him a lot of heartache and the confrontation he must now endure. But he would do what he must to keep Debbie from leaving.

Arriving at White Pines that evening, he felt like a soldier ready to encounter a hail of bullets. Maybe this was a feeling akin to what his grandfather felt on his approach to the beaches of Normandy. Of course, that was totally different — a life-threatening scenario — but Neil's anxiety remained, nonetheless.

At that moment, he saw a nurse locking the doors to her car. He recognized the blond hair, square nose, and thin frame. Exiting his own vehicle, he sank his hands deep into the pockets of his wool coat and approached her. "Trish?"

She whirled. "Huh? What's the matter? What did I do?" She then chuckled. "Oh, it's you. You need to do something about that coat. I thought you were some kind of detective."

"Actually I am. Bet you didn't know that when we first met, did you?" He offered his hand. "Detective Neil Jenson."

At first, she looked stunned. Then a smile crept across her face. "You're no detective. You work with insurance or something."

"I changed occupations for this meeting. This is detective work of the likes you've never seen. Speaking of which, I've heard how my girlfriend is about to get the boot off the floor. All this seems to be coming on the heels of the discussion you and I had the other day."

She began fidgeting with her purse strap.

"I just can't figure out why you would stoop to spreading lies about her and to the head nurse. Are you jealous for some reason?"

Her head jerked around, eyes blazing. "Ha. I am *not* jealous of Debbie, believe me."

"Well, something must not be right to go to these lengths. Unless, of course, you want to tell everyone the truth, which would help in the long run."

"I have," she said, lifting her head high.

Neil felt his irritation rising. "Good. So I

can say for a fact that Debbie isn't getting a transfer, nor will she face any further character assassinations. If things get turned around with your head nurse, I won't make more waves about this whole, sad scenario. If not, then I'd be careful if I were you. Two can play at this game."

"Oh, really? And what can you possibly do to me?" she asked, the uncertainty clearly evident in her voice.

"Just clear things up and keep them clear, Trish. I mean it. Or it's gonna get ugly. I can promise you that."

They stared at each other for a moment before she whirled about and hurried off.

Neil blew out a sigh. *So much for tact.* But, at this point, love was on the line. And he meant what he said. If she got his boiler going any hotter, he was liable to create a firestorm of trouble that would smoke her right out of this place.

He sighed. *One down.* Now he needed to confront the head nurse. Before going up to the third floor, he grabbed a cup of coffee in the cafeteria to ponder the situation. Even with his human frailty, Neil believed God was looking out for him somehow. But as he nursed his cup of coffee, with the steam caressing his face, he wondered if he was only digging a deeper pit for himself and Debbie. There were other ways to deal with such problems — like praying and letting God handle the vindication. He took a swallow of coffee. But he had to do something. How else could he keep Debbie from running? He had to show her he cared. He had to tell her, somehow, that moving away was not the answer, that the real answer for her life could be found only by seeking God's will for her life and, yes, with a guy named Neil by her side. And the best way to do that was to get this Mrs. Whitaker to reconsider, to keep her where she loved the residents like Gram, to make her stay somehow, someway.

"No, I don't think so. Thanks anyway."

Neil cringed as he steered his car onto the highway. His fingers gripped his cell phone. This is what he feared — Debbie giving him the brush-off when he suggested they meet for dinner. The plan was simple enough in his mind — whisk her away to a restaurant and share what was on his heart. But so far, she was not cooperating one iota. How could he display tact in such a situation? He certainly couldn't order her to go out with him. That would send her packing in no time flat.

"So it's final then," he said. "You're moving away?"

"I am looking for another job, if that's what you mean. I made some calls home, and Dad is looking into some possibilities for me. I'm just laying all my options out on the table."

"Good. And I would like to be one of those options. The least you can do is let me take you out to dinner so we can discuss it."

A pause came over the line. "Neil, this just isn't going to work out between us. You know it."

"Look, it's not what you think. That is, I'm not the option. It's what I have to say that is." *Am I making sense?* "There are some things I've discovered that you need to hear. If you aren't willing to look at the big picture, Debbie, then I would say you've grown a bit close-minded."

He could almost feel the coldness seep over the phone line and the, *"I am not!"* ringing loud and clear, though she said nothing. He heard a click and thought she had hung up.

"Okay, I'll go. I won't be labeled close-minded, even if everyone has labeled me a host of other things. You can give your little spiel. It's only fair, I suppose."

He exhaled rapidly. "Good. I'll pick you

up at six." He clicked off his cell phone and shoved it into a small compartment above a used coffee cup. At least he'd convinced her to hear him out. He didn't know what good it would do, but he could try. And if it didn't work out, then God must have other plans for the two of them, though he hated to think what those plans might be.

Debbie wore a different sweater when he arrived to pick her up. A cherry-colored one this time, which poked out from above the jacket she wore. Her face did not bear that soft touch either but appeared stony, with glazed blue eyes to match.

"So where are we going?" she asked. "To the old hangout?"

"No. Somewhere different. My mother always liked this place."

He drove for a time. Debbie stared out the window at the Christmas decorations until her teeth began to chatter. "Do you mind turning on the heat? It's cold in here."

"Of course. Sorry about that. I can think clearer when it's cold."

"No wonder you have to wear a heavy wool overcoat. And black leather gloves. Bet you can see your breath in here." She blew into the air. "Well, now that the heat is on, I don't see it."

Her attitude had definitely changed. It was colder, harsher, like the weather that turned frigid with the arctic blast that roared through just yesterday. How does one warm up a woman chilled by her circumstances?

In another fifteen minutes, he pulled up to a famous country restaurant. "I love this place," Debbie announced.

You hit the bull's eye. Way to go, Neil. He smiled. "Good. Mom always liked to look around the country store inside before they called our name off the waiting list to go into the restaurant."

"Not a very private place to put one's options out on the table," she mused.

"Daleville isn't the best place for a cozy atmosphere. I could take you to Roanoke if you want. Plenty of places there."

"No, this is fine." She immediately left the car and headed into the store. In no time, she immersed herself in the assortment of products for sale. Neil gave the waitress his name and then joined her as she perused handblown glass ornaments, old-fashioned toys, glassware, candles, and everything else women loved to coo over. Just to see Debbie relaxed and enjoying her time of browsing made all this worth his while and more.

Suddenly the waitress called out, "Mr. and Mrs. Jenson, your table is ready."

Debbie whirled, gaping at him.

"I didn't tell her to say that," he said swiftly, feeling the hot flush crawl into his face.

"I sincerely hope that is *not* the option you plan to fork out onto the table."

She laughed loudly as if it were some great joke. They followed the waitress to the rear of the room and, to Neil's relief, a small table tucked away in the corner. So far God was smiling on this little plan of his, minus the Mister-and-Missus routine. Though he did find the idea of being a married couple appealing, in a strange sort of way. He could picture himself spending his life with Debbie. If only she felt the same way. But that was not on his agenda, at least not yet. First things first. He had to make certain she stayed put.

"Get the hash brown casserole," Debbie urged. "You'll love it. By the way, isn't this menu great? It's like being sent back in time, with the old-fashioned parchment paper and writing. And, of course, the good home cooking."

After they gave their orders, Debbie picked up the pegboard puzzle at their table and began playing with it. "I can never leave less than four of these pegs in here," she murmured. "Guess I'm not that smart."

"I think you're very smart." *And beautiful, caring, the perfect match for me . . . if it's God's will for us.*

"Most folks around here wouldn't agree with your assessment of my abilities. In fact, they think I belong somewhere else. Though, at least they haven't yet transferred me off the floor. In fact, Mrs. Whitaker took me off the float list. I wanted to ask her why, but I didn't." She jumped the pegs over each other and tossed them into a small pile.

Neil hid his reaction behind a menu, thanking God silently for small victories.

"Okay, you're hiding something, Neil Jenson."

He glanced over the top of the menu. "Who, me?"

"Yes, you. I can tell. You had something to do with my transfer back to the floor, didn't you? There's no way I could suddenly be back in everyone's good graces without a little help."

"Look, Debbie, I think Mrs. Whitaker realizes the mistake she made. She knows what a positive impact you have on the residents, how well that World War II vet you talk about responds to you. Even Gram went and asked her where you were and why you weren't around, that you were deeply needed and sorely missed. Yep, my grandmother, the crusader. Trish and her crew had convinced Mrs. Whitaker that you were the one causing the problems on the floor, but I think she's beginning to see who the true ringleader is. And I must admit, I think she's a tad bit embarrassed by it all."

"I've worked with her long enough. I can't believe she would take Trish's word over mine."

"Trish has a way about her that is very convincing. I mean, she threw me for a loop about the movie bit. She can be quite the conniver."

"Trish would bite off a hand if it suited her. She doesn't care about anyone, especially the residents. I doubt she'd help a soul unless it was to her advantage, or unless it was a man dressed in a black overcoat and wearing black gloves. She's almost forty, you know, and she wants so badly to be married. I'm just glad you saw through it." Debbie removed a few more pegs. "Hey, I got down to three pegs. I'm getting better at this."

"I'm really sorry work is so tough. But you have to think that God must want something important accomplished in that place, maybe even among those who dislike you. And you can bet when the going gets rough that you must be doing something right. So I hope you'll hang in there and not give up."

The food arrived. Neil prayed for the meal and immediately tackled his hash brown casserole. Debbie only sat there, staring at the food in front of her — the chicken pot-pie with a side dish of hash brown casserole. She made no move to pick up her fork.

Neil immediately tensed. "What's the matter? Are you sick?"

"No." She paused. "Overwhelmed, I guess. I don't know anyone who would stick his neck out for me the way you have. No one I know would go and confront people for my sake. Or buy me dinner in one of my favorite restaurants. And certainly no guy, for that matter. I mean, I've eaten with people before. The girls from church. Things like that. I guess I'm not sure what to say or do at this point."

Neil acknowledged her plate. "C'mon. Enjoy your option then. It's sitting right on the table like you said it would be."

Her forehead wrinkled in confusion. "My option?"

"I'm forking out my option. This is it — dinner out with me. You eat this, and you're stuck here for good. You know it. Skip it and leave, and I guess this really is good-bye."

She stared before a slight smile teased the corners of her lips. "I'm too hungry, and this is simply too good to walk away from." She picked up her fork. "I never thought a way to a woman's heart would be by way of a sweet country restaurant and a man dressed in a black overcoat. But I guess this time it is."

Neil laughed heartily. He never had a more pleasant meal and was sorry to see it end so quickly. But they both had jobs to go to the next morning, and he needed to return to Roanoke. On the drive back to her place, they talked some more. Debbie even broached the topic of his grandfather, Samuel, and asked how things were going in that department.

"I'm at a little bit of a roadblock as far as that's concerned," he admitted. "Maybe it's better that I stop where I am. I should leave the past alone. 'Let it go' like everyone's been telling me to do and concentrate on getting Gram home for a few days over the holidays." Arriving at the apartment building, he wasn't sure if he wanted to let everything go. He had refused to let Debbie go, and through dinner and conversation, she had changed her mind about leaving. But what else could he do? Besides, there were more important things, after all. His life. Debbie's life. And where life was taking them at the moment. And he was glad that they both finally seemed to be heading in the right direction.

"Thanks for dinner. It was great."

"Debbie, I hope you know I care about you. A lot."

She sat still for a moment, pulling the zipper to her jacket up and down. "I know. That's why I couldn't eat my dinner at first. It hit me right then that you really do care what happens to me. It's not just some passing whim. I've gone through that, you know. I thought it was real once, but the guy wanted someone else. My roommate."

"This is *not* some passing fancy. Believe me, it's very real. In fact, I'll even show you how real it can get." He leaned over to kiss her. At first she seemed tense by the encounter. He felt her lips tremble against his. Then she fumbled for the door, and before he knew it, she disappeared into the night.

Startled, Neil flopped back in his seat. Had he made a mistake? Did he move too fast? He only meant it as a kiss of joy, an answer to prayer, and all the proof required to show that they were right for each other.

If only she felt the same way.

CHAPTER 11

Debbie giggled at a singsong rhyme of love trickling through her head, even as she prepared to tackle another day at White Pines. She found it hard to believe all her desires could be realized so quickly and so completely. Never did she think Neil would end the evening the way he had. Reflecting on their past encounters, she could see how much he cared. He wasn't a Brad by any means. He was Neil, his own man, and a wonderful man at that. And no, she wasn't about to leave. Not now, not ever. She could already hear wedding bells pealing, at least in her heart. Maybe one Saturday, she would venture to Roanoke and shop around for a dress. She'd ask her younger sister Kris and some friends from church to be bridesmaids. She would plan out the flowers, the caterer, everything.

She sighed. Forget dreaming about a wedding and then life with Neil in some glorious two-story, four-bedroom home in Roanoke and her with a full-fledged nursing degree, four kids, and a minivan to cart them around in. Time to get back on track, at least for the present. She still had all her Christmas shopping to do and cards to write up. Not to mention her work at White Pines.

Today she was assigned to Harold. He sat in his wheelchair in the usual combat mode, talking about Hitler's Germans and what the troops needed to do to secure victory. "So how are those spies you've been seeing?" he asked Debbie while she combed his hair. "Did you turn them in?"

He remembered their last conversation. "Well, they didn't quite confess, but at least the lies have stopped and the head command has kept me on the unit."

"Yeah, but things can start up again at any moment. Keep alert. And make sure to wear your helmet and keep your gun at the ready, just in case."

Wise words. The Bible talked about keeping one's armament ready when facing the enemies of life. The helmet of salvation, the breastplate of righteousness. The sword of the Spirit or the Word of God, among the other accoutrements.

"They're slick, the enemy," Harold continued. "And they're dug in good up there. They had all that time, you know, to dig in and wait for us to come. It could have been worse. They all thought we would land in Calais, commanded by General Patton." He chuckled. "But we fooled them good. Yep, we sure did, when General Eisenhower moved us to the landing at Normandy."

Normandy. The name triggered something within her, something she had kept buried since the falling-out on the unit and, most recently, Neil's kiss. She recalled the conversation about Neil's true grandfather going off to battle across the ocean. "I know someone who was at Normandy," she said to Harold.

Immediately he perked up. "Was he in my unit? I can't find my buddies anywhere. And Sam, I told you about Sam."

Sam! She began to think. Neil's grandfather was called Samuel. "Did your friend go by Sam or Samuel?"

"Sam, of course. No good man would go by Samuel, 'lessen he was some good ol' boy from back home." Harold laughed and then turned somber. "Poor Sam."

"Tell me about him, Harold."

"He was a great man. A good friend. He had a girl back home. Liv, he called her. And he had a boy, too. Cared about him a lot, he did. Talked about him all the time."

"A boy? How old?"

"Don't recall. Young boy, I think. A few years old. Sam loved that boy. Sent him some letters, I think."

Debbie put the comb away and sat down in a chair. She pulled Harold's wheelchair around to face her. "Harold, what else do you know about Sam? Did you have more than one soldier named Sam serving in your unit?"

"Only one Sam in my unit. But there were heaps more in the division, of course."

"The man I'm thinking about, his name was Samuel Truett. I'm sure you've never heard of him."

A smile spread across the elderly man's face. "Sure I have. That's his name. Sam Truett."

Shock waves rippled through her. She steadied herself. Maybe he was only repeating what she had said. "Did Sam Truett and you go to war, Harold? Was he your friend?"

"Sure. He was my best friend. And he . . ." Harold paused. "Someone get up to the beachhead! Someone's gotta do it. And I can't. I can't face it anymore."

He had lapsed back into his battle state. Somehow the questions had triggered a memory too painful to consider. Harold was

174

again mumbling battle scenarios of Normandy. Yet, the confession coming out of his mouth couldn't help but intrigue Debbie. She didn't know if he was confessing the truth or not, but with this information, Neil might be able to find out on the Internet if the men did, indeed, serve together in the same unit.

Debbie could hardly keep her mind on her work after that. It didn't even bother her that nurses were whispering behind her back, that Trish was dishing out strange looks all day, or even that Mrs. Whitaker looked at her in an odd sort of way during the course of the shift. She could only think of Neil arriving tonight and the news she couldn't wait to share.

On her coffee break, Debbie couldn't wait any longer. Neil had to know what she might have stumbled upon. She sneaked off to a phone booth, placed a call to his cell, and left a message on voice mail, ending with, "I'll wait around for you to come in. I'll be in the cafeteria at four, and I can fill you in on the details then."

All day she waited for his call and his voice exclaiming her news that Harold may have very well known Samuel Truett. The phone stayed strangely silent. She tried not to read anything into it. Certainly the news should have sent him racing to return the call. Maybe he was on a case overload at the insurance company. Or his cell phone wasn't charged up. Or he never checked messages until the end of the day. For whatever reason, the day shift ended with no word from him.

Finally someone notified her she had an outside call. Debbie nearly tripped over a linen cart to answer it at the nurses' station.

"Hey there," Neil said cheerfully. "I got your message. What's up?"

She opened her mouth, ready to spill out everything she had learned concerning Harold. But first, she had to find out something important. "Did your grandma ever have a nickname?"

He laughed. "You mean you called to ask me that? C'mon, Debbie. Why did you really call?"

"No, I'm serious. Did she?"

"Okay, I'll play along, just so long as you're the prize. Grandpa Joe used to call her Liv. Of course we wondered why he would call Gram a name like that. I mean, people 'live,' don't they? Why did he have to call her Liv unless he was glad she was living?" He laughed at his wit.

Debbie could barely catch her breath she was so excited. Harold was telling the truth.

176

He would not know such information unless Samuel Truett once shared it with him. They were all related. It was too unbelievable to be real.

"Do you have a nickname?" he went on, oblivious to the seriousness of this.

She wanted to keep the conversation on topic but decided to wait and reveal her reason for the question when he arrived at White Pines. "Sure. You can call me Sneaky."

"Sneaky. I like that. Why are you sneaking around?"

"Come to White Pines as soon as you can, and I'll tell you."

"Wow, now that's an offer I can't refuse. Be there quick as a flash."

She replaced the receiver, only to find several of the staff giving her inquisitive looks. Didn't anyone believe in privacy anymore? Well, it didn't matter. She knew now she had stumbled upon something extraordinary. *A miracle.* And she couldn't wait to see the look on Neil's face when all was revealed. It would be priceless. If only she had a camera to record all this for posterity's sake. For his children. Maybe *their* children. She tried to steady her breathing and began to pace. She would go see Elvina, but she feared her anxiety would be detected. She would wait for Neil instead.

She checked her watch. He didn't say where he was. For all she knew, he was still hiking it down from Roanoke and she had another forty minutes to wait with the rush hour traffic. Maybe she should just sit in the lounge and read one of the many magazines.

"You seem awfully anxious," the unit secretary noted.

Debbie gave a small smile, realizing she was attracting attention, and strode off to the elevator. She pushed the button. She would wait for him in the lobby. And then she would take him right to where he needed to go.

The doors parted, and suddenly he was there, black overcoat and all, coming toward her. The next moment, she was on the floor, having tripped over her own feet. He looked as startled as she was.

"Wow, what a greeting." Neil offered her his hand.

Debbie winced as the old back wound flared up once again.

"Not your back," he groaned.

"Same place."

"I'm sorry." He shook his head, but his eyes told a different story, one of tender-

178

ness, compassion, and — dare she think it? — love. He gently massaged her upper back in a circular motion. "Let's get some ice on it right away."

"I haven't got time, Neil. This can't wait. I'm dying as it is."

His concern was quickly replaced with confusion. "Huh?"

"There's someplace I have to take you."

"Can't I first say hello to my favorite lady? I promised her I'd be here, and I'm already a little late." He walked off toward Elvina's room, leaving Debbie standing in the hallway. She tried to maintain her composure, but inwardly she felt like a Mexican jumping bean. She began to pace again, even as her back still smarted from the contact with the floor.

"Gram, I think there's something important Debbie needs to tell me," she heard Neil say. "I'll be right back."

Debbie had all she could do to keep from dragging him down the hall. "Neil, I've discovered something really big."

"So have I," he said, pulling her to a stop. His finger traced her cheek and then her lips.

"No, please be serious. This is about your grandfather. Your other grandfather."

His finger dropped. The tender expression

melted away. "I told you I've given up on all that. It's time to move on. 'Let it go,' as everyone's been saying."

Debbie took him by the hand. "No, you can't let this go, believe me. I want you to meet someone."

"I'm not really in the mood for other visitations right now, except with you and Gram."

"You will be, don't worry." As they walked, the words rushed out. "Remember me telling you about Harold? The World War II vet who fought at the Battle of Normandy? Well, he was talking about his best friend in the army. And guess what his name was? Sam! You know, Sam . . . short for Samuel."

"So what? There are plenty of Sams in this world, Debbie."

"I'm telling you, there's a connection." She could see the look of confusion distorting his face as he followed her into the room.

"Hi, Harold," Debbie greeted. "I brought a friend of mine. He's a soldier at heart."

Harold gripped Neil's hand and shook it heartily. "Glad to meet you. We need some strong, young men to join our forces. We have so little. Omaha took everyone away."

Neil cast a sheepish look in Debbie's direction, uncertain how to respond.

"Yes, and guess what, Harold?" Debbie

interjected. "Neil here says he knows Sam, too."

"Really? Wasn't he a great man?"

"I — I know a Samuel Truett," Neil began.

"Sure, Sam Truett. From Wheeling, West Virginia. Were you also in the same unit?"

Neil stared in disbelief. Debbie nudged him. "I, uh, I heard he had a son."

"Sure did. He loved that little boy. Little Albert. He was sure sad to have to leave him." Harold straightened up in his chair. "You know, I saw that little fella before we left. It was raining real hard. Good weather for ducks. I saw them together that day, when they said good-bye."

Neil grabbed for the man's hand, his eyes large. "You saw my dad? And my grandfather? I don't believe it. This is unbelievable. What did they look like? What did they say?"

Harold shrank down in his wheelchair. His bloodshot eyes filled with fear and confusion. "I — I don't know what you're talking about."

Uh-oh, Debbie thought. "Harold, what Neil meant to say is that he knows Sam and Al, also. They were close, too, like family relations, you see."

Harold relaxed when he heard this. "Sam was like a brother to me. He was a tall man.

Bushy dark brown hair, almost looked black, though they made him cut it short. And his boy looked exactly like him."

Debbie glanced at Neil's hair. Wavy hair. Dark brown, nearly black. Excitement bubbled up within her. She wondered if Neil was feeling the same thing, but by the look on his face, he appeared far from it. In fact, he looked ghostly white, as if in a state of shock.

Harold continued chattering about the army and then the Battle of Normandy. All at once, Neil whirled and stumbled out of the room.

"Neil?" She hurried out after him. "What's wrong?"

He glared at her. "How could you put me through that? That man doesn't know my grandfather or my dad. He doesn't even know what year it is. He still thinks he's at Normandy."

"Neil, you're wrong. He knows more than you think. You need to go back and talk to him some more."

"He isn't right in the head, Debbie. I think it's cruel to have planted these things in his mind, only to have him spit them back at me. What do you think this is? A game?"

Debbie stared, horrified. "I never planted anything in his mind. What he's saying is genuine. Besides, I can prove it. He was telling me all about Sam's girl whom he called Liv. The girl he left behind. You were the one who told me your grandmother's nickname was Liv. Harold couldn't have known that fact unless he heard your grandfather, Samuel Truett, say it."

Neil stared into Harold's room where they could hear the man listing off the supplies left after the initial engagement. "This is too unbelievable to be real."

"I know. It's a miracle happening right in this very place. Here is a living link to your grandfather and your past. Please, Neil, go back and talk to Harold. If you don't, you'll regret it the rest of your life."

He considered it for a moment. Slowly he made his way back into the room. Harold had just finished checking the list of first aid supplies on hand and detailing how the medic had been killed. He stopped when he saw Neil. "You're supposed to be on guard duty, young man. What did you say your name was?"

"Neil. Neil Jenson."

"Good-sounding name. I'm Harold White."

"Yes, and you know Sam Truett. Is he . . . is he here? I, uh, I need to talk to him."

The man's lips began to quiver. Tears

filled his eyes. "You didn't hear the news then."

"We, uh, we never got a statement from the War Department, if that's what you mean."

"Fools. They should have told you. You should know. He died right next to me. Right there on the beach. Took a slug in the belly. And he said . . ." He stopped. "Uh-oh. Keep to your feet, men."

Debbie could see the pain of the past driving Harold back into a state of war. She came to his side. "Please, Harold, please tell us what happened to Sam. It will help Neil accept what happened if you tell us. He never got the telegram. Neither did Liv. They need to know."

"Liv doesn't know either? Sam talked about her with his dying breath. Told me to tell her that he loved her."

"She wants to see him. It's her Christmas wish."

Harold's head dropped to his chest.

Debbie heard a noise she hadn't anticipated. Weeping.

"Sh–she won't see him no more. He's gone. And she — she will have to take care of Sam's little boy. I'm sorry, Sam. I know I promised you, and I'm sorry." He lifted his face, damp with tears, and looked at Neil.

"I'm sorry, young man. I told Sam I would take care of Liv and the boy. On his dying breath, I promised. But I didn't. I didn't do what I said I would do. When the war was over, I came home and did nothing. I didn't even check to see how Albert was doing." Great heaves shook his frail form. "I'm sorry, Sam."

Neil ventured forward and took the feeble man in his arms. Unresolved grief filled them both. Debbie looked on, the tears bubbling in her own eyes, as Neil embraced the closest link to both the grandfather and the father he never knew.

CHAPTER 12

"If that wasn't a bomb falling out of the skies, I don't know what is."

Debbie couldn't help but agree with Neil's assessment of the encounter with Harold White. They decided on a drive to look at Christmas lights for a change of pace but were really using the occasion to mull over everything. Though shocking, she recognized the news provided answers Neil desperately needed. And she was glad for it. Neil had a living testimony of one who witnessed his roots.

"I'm amazed that Harold actually knew him," Neil went on. "That they were best friends, of all things. That he saw my grandfather die there on the beach. What do you wager the odds are of such an occurrence?"

"A million to one at least. Which is why this has to be God's doing."

He began tapping on the steering wheel. "I can see why God tells us not to worry about tomorrow, that it will take care of itself. He orchestrates the future. I could never have brought all this together. Think of all the minute details that had to come forth to make this reunion work. For instance, if you hadn't taken that tumble in the road, none of this would've happened."

Debbie chuckled, even as her hand went to her battered tailbone. "I guess this is one time I can say a bruise on the backside was worth it."

Suddenly she saw one of his large hands sneak over and take hold of hers; then he gave a gentle squeeze.

"And I'm happy, too, that you decided not to move away. I would've never discovered the truth. You've made such a difference in my life, Debbie. I can't begin to say."

"Please don't put me on a pedestal. Remember, Mrs. Whitaker thought I was the worst thing to come storming onto the floor."

"She didn't know what a good nurse she had. And that's what I told her, plain and simple. That she should be proud to have you there, caring about the residents more than all of her staff combined. That you gave your life to them every day. And she owed you big-time."

"Boy, I'll bet that went over like a lead

balloon. Neil's good-hearted tact." She giggled.

He laughed in response. "Hey, she listened. And she stopped sending you off to other floors. I know Gram is very glad to have you back." He gave her hand another gentle squeeze. "So am I. I was miserable when we were apart. I couldn't sleep or eat." He paused.

The symptoms sounded familiar to her. No appetite. Loss of sleep. Could it be the symptoms of that sickness called love? She sucked in her breath, at a loss for words.

"And now I need you more than ever."

She looked at his hand, still curled around hers, and wondered what he meant. As a companion? His one and only? She sucked in her breath, suddenly nervous. Were all her fantastic dreams about to come to pass? If so, was she ready to handle them?

"Somehow we're going to have to break the news to Gram about Harold and this Sam Truett fellow. Well, I guess he isn't just some fellow down the street. He was my grandfather. But she needs to know the truth. It's been her wish to find out what happened to him. I know it will hardly be a great Christmas gift, but maybe she can find some peace, after all is said and done."

Debbie blew out a sigh. He hadn't said

what she thought he would say, but then again, maybe it was for the better. She didn't think she was yet ready for dreams to come true anyway. "So how do you plan on springing the news?"

"I'm not sure. I was hoping you'd be able to give me some ideas. If I just came out and said it, she might not believe me. Then we'd be in real trouble."

Debbie had little time for contemplation as they slowed to a stop behind a row of cars lined up along the road. Up ahead, she saw colored lights and oversized glimmering snowflakes hovering in midair. She lowered the window and strained to see. "Neil, you won't believe this, but there's a house down the road here that has every kind of light display imaginable."

"Must be something big. The traffic has come to a dead halt."

They inched their way forward until they came to a large sign welcoming all visitors, and an arrow pointed to where cars could park in a farmer's field. Debbie nodded to Neil's inquiry as to whether or not they should investigate. He turned into the field and parked. "This is great," she squealed. "You'll get to share in a family tradition. The house is decorated up like the one I described to you when I was a kid."

"I'll gladly look at any tradition that has to do with you. Let's go see what this is all about."

Debbie stared in amazement at the displays — at least six different lighted Nativity scenes, snowflakes positioned high up in the trees, dancing bears, tin soldiers, a huge train, and so many more it nearly took her breath away. They walked through lighted tunnels, past Mary and Joseph looking upon the newborn Babe. They strolled along a pebbled path to a tiny house that held at least a hundred animated Santas, carolers, angels, and music boxes, all playing carols with glee.

"A genuine Christmastown, USA," Neil commented. "I'd love to see their electric bill."

"These people do love Christmas," she agreed. Walking by the main house, Debbie gazed upon the dozens of lighted roses on the ground like a winter's garden. "Beautiful."

"Seeing this, I can't help thinking about Gram," Neil said. "She would get a kick out of it all. She loves light displays. I want her to have a nice Christmas, but I don't know if I can pull it off. And now we're going to have to break the news to her about my grandfather."

"It will work out fine, don't worry," she said, drawing closer to his coat, which felt better than any security blanket. "Look over there."

Her sights fell on a large tent where inside a band played lively tunes. They looked at each other and walked over to find people sitting in folding chairs, clapping away to gospel tunes praising God. At a large table, an older woman offered hot chocolate and Christmas cookies.

"You have quite a setup here," Neil remarked.

"We do it every year. We like to bless the community."

"It must take you all year to put up the lights and take them down again."

She laughed. "We start in early fall. And usually it takes until the end of January to tear it all down. We have several sheds in the back where we store it all. But we love doing it." She nodded toward the band. "This way, people will also stop by the tent here and learn something about God."

"Interesting," Neil said, taking a seat beside Debbie to hear the band. "They set up all these lights to draw people in, and then arrange to have a band play gospel songs and talk about the real reason for the season. What a great way to minister to the

191

people."

"I'd love to do something like this one day," Debbie mused. "But I would do my place up entirely in white lights. I'd serve cinnamon stars. And mulled cider."

Neil snickered. "You'll have to marry a guy who likes to do that kind of stuff."

Debbie looked down at the steaming hot cocoa she held in her hands. How she hoped Neil, sitting there in his black wool coat, might be that kind of guy.

"I'm lucky if I can even screw in a lightbulb," he added.

For some reason, the comment saddened her. Maybe she had been living in a cloud these days since they shared a kiss, convinced that God had brought the right man into her life. Or was she only caught up in some emotional whim and not seriously thinking and praying about this? Of course Neil had many special characteristics that appealed to her. The way God brought them together through his grandmother had been a miracle, as well. "You were good at untangling that strand of lights in my apartment," she remarked.

He laughed. "Yes, I did do a pretty good job. Maybe there's hope for me in the decorating department, after all."

Debbie hoped so, too, as a rousing rendition of "Amazing Grace" filled the tent. The music followed them out into the wintry night. Again Debbie felt Neil's thickly gloved hand slip around hers. They walked toward the car and gazed upon the many lighted forms of forest animals tucked back in the woods.

"There really has been amazing grace in my life," Neil said, staring at the animated deer that nodded their heads as if in agreement to what he said. "All grace. Grace to figure out this thing with my grandparents. Grace for my desk job. Grace to get through the latest fiasco at White Pines with the nurses. Grace on my family. Grace to know more about you, Debbie, and make sure I don't ignore any of your instructions ever again. And grace to remember that tact is the key." He chuckled.

She sighed. *God, how can this man not be for me? He must be. He knows You so well. Look what we've been through. Even when I wanted to leave, he remained steadfast, firm, unrelenting. I will even teach him how to string up white lights, if only You would finish this work in us.*

When she opened her eyes, he was gazing at her intently. She thought perhaps he might kiss her, but the moment passed. Neil coaxed her toward the car. She sighed. It was better for them to travel the road of love one step at a time, to wait on God's leading and not act out of impulsiveness.

Once inside the car, Neil sat in his seat as if frozen, staring out the window.

"What are you thinking about?" she asked.

"The work I have to do. Like telling Gram the news, which I hope doesn't shock her to death."

"Neil, we'll sleep on it tonight and see if we have any ideas on how to tell her. I know when we do come up with an idea, it will be perfect."

"Debbie, you're something else."

A kiss of gratitude followed in the most perfect moment possible. As far as she was concerned, her Christmas wish had already come, wrapped in a big black wool overcoat, and with a future waiting to be had. There was no better fulfillment to a season of giving and joy.

"Please?"

The elderly woman shook her head and looked away.

"But, Gram, you need to talk to him."

She shook her head again. "I'm not speaking about private things to some man I don't even know. Really, Nathaniel. How can you even suggest such a thing?" She

194

drew up her lap robe as if to guard herself.

Neil felt his frustration level rising. He glanced back at Debbie who nodded her head, her eyes wide, as if encouraging him to stand firm. "Gram, this is the only way. Believe me. I talked to him. He knows everything. Even your nickname. How would he know that unless he knew Sam? Your Sam? Sam Truett."

"Nathaniel, you don't live here. I hear things all the time. The poor people calling out for loved ones. One lady asking for her cat. They have lost their minds, many of them. And I'm not about to trust something this personal, this dear to me, to some crazy old man." Her voice heightened. "Anyway, I don't want to get to know any more men. I had two men, and they both left me alone to live in this place. So please don't force me to meet some crazy man."

Neil retreated into the hall. He felt sick to his stomach, even as Debbie laid her soothing hand on his shoulder. "What am I going to do? She won't talk to Harold. I guess we are similar in a way, even if we aren't blood relations. I didn't want to talk to the man either, at first. But it was the best thing I ever did."

"We can't force her, Neil. Maybe she's afraid to face the truth. It's scary confronting the past. Let it go."

He began to chuckle scornfully. " 'Let it go.' Honestly, if I hear that statement again, I think I'll go crazy." He'd no sooner spoken than regret seized him. "I'm sorry," he said to Debbie. "But this is something I've just got to see through." He turned on his heels and started to walk down the hall. When Debbie asked where he was going, he told her he was going to think. He spoke the truth, but he also wanted to see that man again. Harold. The man who knew his grandfather. The one who knew his father. The only living, breathing link left to his past.

He brushed by the nurses, many of whom only gave him a passing glance. He was glad for small miracles. Word had spread about him and Debbie being an "item," and it made him happy. Now, if he could just resolve this situation, it would be a merry Christmas all the way around.

He arrived at the open doorway of Harold's room to find Trish standing inside, scolding Harold as she tried to make him sit properly in his wheelchair.

"Who do you think you are, talking to him like that?" Neil snarled.

Trish whirled around, her face white.

"You don't deserve to work here. It's an

honor to work with people like him. You treat them like they're dirt on the floor."

She said nothing but only stared. Even Harold stared, his eyes wide.

"You know, if you can't do a job right, you shouldn't be doing it. These people deserve better. You should be giving them all the respect they can get. Now please leave."

Trish said nothing but hurried out of the room. Harold shook his head in wonder. "I would promote you if I had the authority, young man."

Neil pulled up a chair and sat down beside him. "Do you remember me, Harold?" He saw the tears of recognition.

"W–Why did you come back?"

"I need a favor. A big one."

"I . . . uh . . ." Harold stared off into the distance. "Hey, I see them. Here they come!"

Neil gently took the man's face in his hands, turning it so their eyes met. "Harold, it's time to face reality. The war's long over, and now I need your help."

"I can't help you."

"Yes, you can. You knew my grandfather, Sam Truett. You knew my dad, Albert, when he was a little boy. You can help me in more ways than you know. You already saved me from an enemy of confusion and all the unanswered questions. Now you can save a woman who has been living with questions all her life. You can fulfill her one wish at this moment."

"But . . . I don't know any women."

"Liv. You can help Liv."

His wrinkled hand gripped Neil's. "Liv! You mean, she's here?"

"Yes, she lives here. Down the next hall. A miracle of God, really. She's Sam's Liv, the one he talked about on the battlefield, the woman who took care of Sam's little boy. And I'm that little boy's son."

Harold began to tremble. "It can't be. You can't be."

"Harold, I am. And right now I need you to go talk to Liv. I need you to tell her what happened to Sam that day on the beach. Let her heart rest in peace."

He shook his head. "I can't do that."

"Look, I know what you said. How you made Sam a promise when he lay there dying. You think you didn't live up to it. But now is the time. You can fulfill the promise to Sam by meeting Liv and telling her the truth. Don't you think Sam would want her to know what happened to him?"

"But he wanted me to take care of them. And I didn't. I did nothing. I came home and tried to forget."

"Harold, you have to let that go." Neil nearly laughed at his use of the expression — *let it go.* But maybe there was more to the saying than met the eye. "Now you can do something, something really big, to put Liv's heart at rest. She told me the best Christmas present she could have was to know what happened to Sam. And you're the one who can make it happen."

Harold sat there, seemingly frozen in place in his wheelchair. At least he was no longer murmuring words of war, seeing the enemy, talking of bullets and death. For the first time, he was not immersing himself in the past but facing it.

"All right."

"What?" Neil could hardly believe what he heard.

"I'll talk to Liv and tell her that I knew Sam and what happened to him. Where is she?"

Neil brushed his hand across his face, unsure if this was real. "Wow, Harold. Okay." His thoughts became muddled. "Look, I'll try to set up a meeting place, okay? You two should have privacy. I'll get back to you."

Harold shook his hand. "You grew up to be a nice young man," he said. "Sam would be proud. In fact, you look like him."

Neil couldn't hold the tears that teased his eyes. He was his father's child and his grandfather's grandson. A part of both men lived on. He felt proud then, proud to be a product of men like that. He only prayed the life he lived would preserve their honor.

CHAPTER 13

"How do you think it went?" Debbie wondered.

Neil tried hard not to let his nervousness show, even as his skin crawled with prickles of anxiety and curiosity. He picked up a travel mug of coffee. He didn't even want to wager a guess. As it was, he'd convinced Gram to go to the meeting on a slightly false pretense, telling her that a friend from long ago had come to see her. Now he wondered if he'd made yet another awful mistake. Maybe he should have come right out and told her. But if he had, he was certain she would have refused the encounter. This was the only way.

"You aren't saying anything."

He took another gulp of the stale coffee before tucking the mug into the car's cup holder. "I don't know. I guess I'm trying not to think about it too much. I just hope and pray I haven't made the worst mistake of my life by having the two of them meet. If this ends up killing Gram, I'll never forgive myself."

Immediately Debbie put her hand on his, steadying his nervous tremors. "Neil, please don't say that. We need to believe that everything is going to work out right. We didn't come this far to let it all go downhill. God knows your heart, that you want good to come from a situation that has been going on now for over sixty years."

"No matter how this ends, I plan to visit Harold as much as I can. The man is my relative, even if he is not a blood relation. He's my only living link, besides Gram, to my grandfather and my father. He deserves all the attention I can give him, and so much more, really."

"I'm sure he'll love having you for an adopted grandson. I think it will do wonders for him. And it will do wonders for your grandmother, too."

Neil tried hard not to fidget while he glanced out the car window. He had wanted to go back and be with Gram after the meeting was all said and done, but he was glad he hadn't. Better to give Gram time after something of this magnitude. He only hoped their close relationship as grandmother and grandson still remained intact.

"Hello?" Debbie whispered in his ear. "You okay?"

"Yeah. I guess we gave the best medicine we could. Now we have to wait for the healing."

She nodded before planting a light kiss on his cheek. "I agree. Maybe you can rest easier tonight, knowing all this is finally out in the open."

"I hope so." That would be a nice change to a Christmas season that had begun in ways he never could have imagined. He glanced over at Debbie. Her eyes were wide, cheeks all aglow, a vision of beauty during a difficult and unpredictable time. He was glad to have her by his side, and he hoped she'd stay forever.

"So let's change the subject and concentrate on our job for today. Did you bring your Christmas shopping list?" Debbie reached inside her pocket and pulled out a sheet of paper filled with scribbles.

Neil shrugged.

"You don't have one? Then how are you supposed to remember who to buy for and what?"

Lists. They were as foreign to him as picking up a dust rag and cleaning the apartment. He usually relied on his brain to do the remembering, but these days, his mind felt more like a colander, with ideas dripping into oblivion. "I'll see what you buy, and maybe it will give me some hints."

When Debbie suggested a shopping trip to Roanoke to while away the hours on this Saturday afternoon, Neil thought it a good idea. He felt the need for an escape, and Debbie was a good distraction — until he found himself thinking again about Christmas and all the great ideas he had still not put into motion. He hadn't talked to his mother about inviting Gram home for the holidays, nor had he looked into another private-duty nurse to replace Trish. With the weight of the grandfather issue, it had taken a backseat.

"Don't worry about the list," Debbie went on. "We'll make one right now. You tell me who you need to buy for, and maybe I can make a suggestion." She took out a scrap of paper and a pen from her purse.

"Gram," he began. "I still need a private-duty nurse."

"You mean you haven't gotten one yet? Neil, you can't leave important things like that to the last minute. As it is, it's probably too late."

"So there's no chance of you doing it? What if you called in sick? Or said that a loved one needed special care over the holidays?"

The look she gave communicated her answer, though he hoped a miracle might still be in the works. When she launched into getting docked a week's pay for not showing up on Christmas, along with the horror of telling a lie to boot, he immediately retreated. Maybe with all the turmoil brewing this year, he should just forget about inviting Gram to Mom's house. But the more he considered dropping the idea, the less peace he felt. It seemed perfect having her there with all his siblings together, especially after the Harold incident. His aunts and uncles would stop by for hors d'oeuvres on Christmas Eve. It would be like a reunion. Gram would have a ball, holding newborn great-nieces and great-nephews, seeing her great-grandchildren, laughing, and reminiscing about the old days. He wanted to make it work, but so far, nothing was falling into place the way he'd intended.

He put his thoughts aside then and made small talk about gift ideas for others in the family. When they arrived, the mall in Roanoke was fairly bursting at the seams with shoppers. Once inside, they paused at several stores to do some window-shopping.

Fuzzy sweaters like the kind Debbie wore graced the mannequins. Neil wondered if she would like another one for her wardrobe. Did she own a black one? He liked black. Or was a sweater too personal? Maybe he should stick to old-fashioned notepaper in a flowered box. Or a large potted poinsettia. A bouquet of red roses better illustrated his heart. A diamond ring would be the ultimate gift, if he thought she would say yes. She had to say yes. They had been through so much. She had seen the inner struggles of his heart and the goings-on with his family. She had become a crucial part of his life. They were being knit together as one.

A poke in his arm drew him back to the reality of the shopping experience. Debbie had stopped at some bath boutique. Flowery scents assaulted his senses. Looking across the way, he saw a computer store. That was more his style. He was curious to know what new games would be out for the coming New Year. Maybe he could find something for his brother, Dick.

"I think you can find some nice stuff in here for your mother and sister." She poked him again. "And stop thinking about buying yourself a computer game," she said with a teasing tilt.

"I can't get anything past you, can I?" He smirked and followed her inside. There wasn't a guy in the place, only women perusing the multitude of soaps and lotions in every color of the rainbow. The warring scents assaulted his nostrils.

Debbie opened a bottle of pink stuff and placed it under his nose. "Isn't this nice?"

"Smells like a lollipop. What is it?"

"It's called Raspberry Dream. You really don't seem into this."

"Tell you what . . ." He took out his wallet and pulled out a few bills. "Why don't you buy my mom and Sandy something for me? I'm no good at this kind of stuff. To me, everything smells the same."

"You aren't leaving me for that computer store across the way, are you?"

"No. I was hoping to check my voice mail for any messages. Here," he said, handing the cash to Debbie, "you can spend up to fifty bucks on each."

"Wow! Okay." Debbie looked as though he had given her the key to the bank. She grabbed a shopping basket and began performing the sniff test on various products.

Neil moseyed outside the store, took out his cell phone, and hit the auto-dial button to access his messages.

"Neil, this is Mom. I just got a call from the charge nurse at White Pines. Elvina isn't doing very well. She won't take her pills for the nurse. Maybe you can go over there and see what's happening. I'll try to see her tonight."

His hand tightened around the phone. *What? How can that be?* It didn't sound like Gram at all.

He listened to the next message.

"Neil? This is Trish from the White Pines Health Care Facility. I'm calling about your grandma. We've been having a hard time getting her to take anything. She won't eat or even take her medications. Everyone here is very concerned. If she doesn't take her pills soon, she may be transferred to the hospital. Please give the floor a call back. You can ask for Mrs. Whitaker."

Even Trish was calling? A chill fell over him, despite the warmth of the mall and the fact that he was perspiring heavily inside his wool sweater. A message from the head nurse, Mrs. Whitaker, followed, echoing her concern over Gram's condition.

Neil hurried back inside the store to find Debbie carrying two gift baskets full of bath products. "Hey, Neil, how about gift baskets? Don't they look nice?" Her cheerful face deteriorated into one of concern.

"What's the matter?"

"Tell you in a minute. Go ahead and get them. We have to go." He waited until she paid and handed him the change. "Gram is refusing to take everything. Food, pills." He swept his hand across his face.

"Neil, I'm so sorry!"

He took the bags. "This is it, Debbie. She's going to die. Grandpa Joe's gone. My dad's gone. Now this whole Sam and Harold story. I guess she thinks she has nothing left to live for. She's given up."

"Neil, we have to pray that won't happen," she said as they hurried toward the escalator. "God isn't going to let anything or anyone take her until it's time. You have to believe that."

"Maybe this is the time." He bumped the shopping bags into the door in his haste to leave. Outside, the parking lot was filled to capacity with last-minute shoppers. "This is a nightmare. How am I going to get out of here?"

"Neil, it will be okay."

Debbie appeared so calm, cool, and collected. Maybe if it were her flesh-and-blood relative in dire straits, she would act differently. She, too, would be angry at the shoppers and traffic, realizing she was still an hour away from a loved one ready to sink into eternity without even saying good-bye.

"I should have never set up that meeting between her and Harold," he said gruffly, trying to pull out of the parking spot. Debbie warned him about an oncoming car. "I see it. This is nuts. We're never going to get there in time. She'll die, and it's my fault."

"No, it isn't your fault, Neil Jenson. So stop it right now."

The tone of her voice made him stare at her in surprise. He managed to steer the car out of the parking lot and to the main road heading for the interstate. "I don't know, but it's obvious things aren't resolved. And now she's doing this, like she's decided to take revenge or something."

"So they told you she isn't eating?"

Neil nodded. "Yeah, and not taking her pills. Her refusal to take her blood pressure medication has me worried. She could have a stroke if her blood pressure isn't in check. She's already had a mild one, you know. A few years back." He then muttered about the crazy drivers. "This is nuts." He abruptly rolled down his window. "Hey, how would you like me to cut you off?" he shouted at a driver in the passing lane.

Debbie sank down in her seat and stared out the window.

Neil frowned. He knew he was acting like

a wild man, controlled by anxiety and confusion, guilt and blame. He didn't know what to say or how to react. His emotions were doing all the talking. But maybe Debbie needed to witness the raw side of him — see that he wasn't all dapper and kind, helping his elderly grandmother, being a hero. He had his share of faults and problems, too. He was a regular flesh-and-blood guy, not some stained glass saint.

He began to grind his teeth as negative thoughts drove away peace, joy, and faith to some black void of nothingness. Debbie reached over and inserted a CD. Christmas carols filled the car. He tried to listen to them, but all he could envision was Gram, pale as a ghost, her hand lying across her chest, her breathing ragged as she spoke her final words.

I'm dying, Nathaniel. Now that everyone I love is gone, I might as well see them in heaven. Kiss the family for me. Tell them there's nothing more they can do for me.

"Neil, watch out. You're driving on the shoulder."

Neil quickly brought the car back onto the highway. Gram had sometimes refused to eat, but never had he known her not to take her blood pressure medication or any of the other colorful pills she took each day and night. She was trying to make herself die.

"I won't have her committing suicide," he growled out loud.

"Neil?"

"She's trying to kill herself. Keeping herself from medication. As a Christian woman, she should know that's wrong."

Debbie scraped tiny images with her fingernail into the frost forming on the window. Two hearts intertwined. A star. A candle. A mural of Debbie's mind began materializing on the window. "Neil, she's acting out on her feelings. A cry for help, you might say. This is a tough time of year for the residents. We just need to take it one step at a time and not go in there looking to condemn her. Something is making her do this. If we can find out the reason, we might be able to deal with it." Now she set to work on a small stable, no doubt the beginnings of the Nativity.

In no time, they were on the road headed for White Pines. Neil wasn't sure what to say or do when he arrived. He knew Debbie was right, that he needed to keep his opinions in check. He couldn't march right in there and force-feed Gram the pills, though he might be tempted to do so if necessary.

He ran into the facility with Debbie trying

in vain to keep up. He didn't even notice until he entered the elevator and pushed the button that he'd left her behind. His thoughts were on one person and one person alone. When he exited, the head nurse was standing there next to the medication cart. From the look on her face, the news was not good.

"Mr. Jenson, I'm sure you're here about your grandmother."

"Is she dying?"

"I wouldn't say that. But if she keeps going the way she is, it's not looking good. I was going to put in calls to your other relatives. Since you're the one who sees her so much and your name is listed first on the chart, I wanted to wait until you came in. But I will be obliged to share the information with her power of attorney, a Mr. Kevin Jenson."

"He's her oldest living son. So what brought this on?"

"I was hoping you could tell me. She seemed perfectly fine a few days ago, and suddenly this happened. Not that I want to pry into personal matters, but I hope everything is all right. I know disagreements can happen from time to time."

"Actually there was a wake-up call of sorts." He described in abbreviated detail the scenario surrounding his real grand-father, Gram's first beau, and how Harold knew him from the war.

"Isn't that amazing? I would think Elvina would be happy to hear such news. To know that there's a resident right on this floor who was so close to your family."

"I guess it did the opposite. Now she feels there's nothing left to live for."

Mrs. Whitaker nodded in sympathy. "I'm so sorry. You realize if she doesn't take her pills we may have to transfer her to the hospital. As it is, her blood pressure is beginning to spike. And she needs fluids."

The mere mention of all this made him sick inside. "I'll get her to take her pills," he said with a huff. He came to the doorway where Gram lay in bed, her eyes closed, looking like a pale doll. It didn't seem possible that she had been reduced to a feeble state in such a short period of time.

When he came to her bedside and spoke, her eyelids fluttered open. Her gray blue eyes stared straight ahead. "I know why you're here, Nathaniel, but it's my decision. You've made your decision. I've made mine."

"It isn't your decision, Gram. Not when it comes to life and death. That's God's decision."

Her cheek muscles tightened. "Nathaniel, I won't debate this with you."

"Gram, you've just had the greatest encounter with a man who knew Sam and was with him when he died. Harold's the last living person Sam talked to. The one who heard Sam's last words, and they were all about you. Isn't that worth something?"

"You might have at least told me who it was I was meeting and not some fancy story about an old friend from long ago. You lied to me, Nathaniel."

He hadn't lied. Harold was a friend from the past, a very good friend of Sam's. "I knew you wouldn't have met him if I told you everything. You have to admit it's a miracle, Gram. That a man living on the very same floor as you knew Samuel Truett."

"Harold is a very nice man. And I appreciate what he had to say, even if I think he made it up."

"He isn't making it up. He even knew your nickname because Samuel told him. So, Gram, there's no reason to do this to yourself. None at all."

"I've made my decision. I want to be home with my dear Joe."

"This isn't your decision to make. Life-and-death decisions are in the hands of the

Lord. He's the One who decides. You do this, and you're playing God."

She closed her eyes. "Please leave. I want to rest."

"You can't do this. Think about your family." *And me,* he added silently.

"I have thought of my family. And who really cares anyway? None of them come to see me, except for you. I have been more of a burden than anything. You know it, and so do I. There really isn't anything more to say."

Neil stood there speechless. What was he supposed to do? He couldn't make the family come see her. But he had visited her. Didn't that matter to her? Didn't all that count? He wanted to shout, to make her see reason, to tell her how selfish this all was. He thought about putting on a record to calm the situation, but right now he needed something more powerful. Something that would speak louder than mere human words could say. He picked up her Bible. "Can I read you a few verses, Gram?"

She shrugged. At least she didn't order him to leave and never come back. He clung to any signs of hope at this crucial time. Flipping through the scriptures, he prayed for a word to minister to her heart. He cleared his throat. "I've always liked these verses, Gram, in Proverbs, chapter three, especially when I'm trying to figure out things in my life.

" 'Trust in the Lord with all your heart and lean not on your own understanding; in all your ways acknowledge him, and he will make your paths straight. Do not be wise in your own eyes; fear the Lord and shun evil. This will bring health to your body and nourishment to your bones.' "

He looked up to see Gram's eyelids beginning to close from fatigue. With a sigh, he shut the Bible, placed it on her bedside table, and whispered good-bye. He had done all he could. The rest was up to God. Exiting the room, he nearly stumbled into Trish. She appeared to be lingering in the hallway. She said nothing but pretended to arrange her linen cart. He glanced back to see Trish enter another room across the hall. Neil wondered if she had been eavesdropping. What did it matter? Gram wanted to die. He might as well leave here and never come back, for what good he seemed to do. Nothing was working out, no matter what he did.

Neil never felt so burdened. He strode down the hall, and suddenly he was in front of Harold's room. He peeked inside. Harold had wheeled his chair into the bathroom and was combing his hair. To Neil's amazement, the veteran was singing a song. He stared in disbelief. How could the man look so alive when only a week ago he seemed confused and out of his mind? And now Gram was the one acting confused. *It's like they switched places.* The sight of the man, renewed in spirit, cheered Neil immensely. Finally some good fruit to be had after weeks of bad.

"Harold?" he said softly, stepping inside.

Harold wheeled his chair around. "Neil. I'm glad to see you. Come in."

It felt good to be acknowledged in such a friendly manner. He sat down slowly in a chair.

"You don't look too good," Harold observed. "What's wrong?"

"It's Gram. Liv, that is."

"What's the matter? Is she sick?"

"She won't take her medicine. Her blood pressure is rising. She's decided it's her time to die."

He twisted his face. "Is it because of me?" He said it matter-of-factly but with innocence and vulnerability. Tears welled up in his stark gray eyes. "It is because of me, isn't it? Because I didn't take care of her and Albert. She won't forgive me. That's why she's doing this."

"No, Harold. It's a bunch of different things. She's decided to feel sorry for herself and doesn't care about the consequences. Maybe you could talk to her again."

Harold shook his head. "I don't see what good that will do. As it is, I'm responsible. She was fine until . . . until . . ." He began to mumble something under his breath.

"No. She's lonely, and I don't think she knows what she's truly lonely for. I can't fulfill her needs, even though I come to visit. No one can. Only God can fulfill them, whether here in White Pines or in her own house. But it's hard convincing her of that. Gram's lived through a lot of loss. Maybe it's finally caught up with her. I know you've been through a lot, too. That's why I think you can reach her when no one else can."

"But I wouldn't know what to say or what to do. I talked to her once already. It didn't seem to do much good."

"Sometimes the best thing you can do is nothing at all. Maybe you can just sit there for starters. Let her know someone else cares in this world besides me. Let her see God through you."

Harold turned back to the bathroom mirror, staring at his reflection. "I suppose I could sit there for a little while anyway."

Neil breathed a sigh of relief. He helped

wheel Harold down the hallway, past the curious onlookers who had gathered at the nurses' station. Trish stared at them as if this were some kind of evolving soap opera. Neil brought Harold to the doorway of Gram's room.

Harold said nothing, only stared at the woman lying in bed with her eyes closed. Neil saw his dry, cracked lips begin to move. Harold was praying! The sight of it moved Neil as well as convicted him. *'Pray without ceasing.' Harold is right. Pray when the going gets rough. Pray and don't stop. God, please make this work out all right. You saved me. You helped my family by revealing a secret from so long ago. You helped me by bringing Debbie into my life and blessing our developing relationship. Please save my grandma.*

CHAPTER 14

"I don't know why you're here."

"You know why I'm here. Your grandson even said so. He says you aren't eating or taking your medicine. You have to eat."

"It doesn't matter. No one cares. Once they leave you in this place, that's the end. Sometimes people come to visit. But really, we are just a burden to everyone."

Silence weighed the air.

Debbie's skin began to crawl. Harold and Elvina were in the room talking, but she couldn't help overhearing. Neil's heart would break if he knew what they were talking about. Thankfully he was gone. She had heard, of course, how Neil talked to Harold yesterday, convincing him to meet with Elvina. Harold had come, but she refused to see him. Now today, by some miracle, she had agreed to a visit. "One last time," as she put it, "before I leave this world. There's nothing worth living for anyway."

But there is, despite the situation, Debbie thought. God was an ever-present help in times of need. He remained in control, even at White Pines. He cared. His love knew no bounds, whether in a house or here in a facility. And it was God to whom people needed to look to for comfort and consolation. If only she knew how to convey these things so despair didn't rule the night. She had had to learn it well herself when she thought despair would overcome her. She was a living example. No one was immune, whether they lived on the outside looking in or the inside looking out. And through it all, she discovered He was sufficient for everything, in every situation.

"That may be," Harold continued to Elvina, "but it still doesn't give you the right to hurt yourself and others, like Neil for example. He's done a lot for you. He's given up his life for you. And what have you done?"

"Why! I never."

"In the army, it was considered the worst kind of cowardice to harm yourself just so you could get out of the war. And that's what you're doing here, Liv."

"This isn't some kind of battlefield, Harold."

"Maybe you don't think so, but it sure

can be. The same evil I fought long ago is still around. Sin don't go away. It's still the same. There's no difference in God's eyes. Sin is still sin, whether it's Hitler killing God's people or you wanting to kill yourself. And the problem is, you'll end up hurting a lot of other people if you do. Nothing is worth that, no matter where you end up living out your life. And here there are nice people, kind people helping you and loving you, like Neil and Debbie and even that head nurse there. So don't be so selfish. Think about other people besides yourself for a change."

Debbie could hardly believe this was the same Harold who spoke such words. It was like he had awakened from some kind of coma after all this time and now was speaking righteous words full of life-changing power.

Just then she felt a breeze and turned to see Trish rolling her linen cart along. "Playing matchmaker?" she asked with a teasing lilt to her voice.

Debbie picked up a pillowcase from her linen cart, pretending to fold it. "Hardly. But it's nice to see the change in Harold."

Trish paused to observe the two residents having a conversation with one another. "Wonder of wonders. And Harold doesn't think Elvina is some enemy soldier either."

"That's because he knows her. Indirectly, that is. Harold knew a man who was close to Elvina before the war. His name was Sam. Harold and Sam fought side by side in Normandy. Harold was there when Sam got shot and took his last breath. Elvina never knew what happened to Sam — that is, until now, sixty years later." Debbie drew in a breath.

Trish stared, her mouth forming a circle. "So you mean Elvina had another husband named Sam?"

"Sam was like her boyfriend, I guess you could say, before she got married. He was a widower with a small son when they met. I think his wife died in childbirth. Anyway he wanted Elvina to take care of his little boy while he was away in the army. He never came home. Elvina adopted the boy and made him a part of the family even after she married her husband, Joe. That adopted boy turned out to be Neil's father. That's why Neil calls her his grandmother to this day, even though there is no blood relation."

Trish stood transfixed. "This is too weird."

"Yes. It's a miracle."

She hesitated. "I know what it's like to be adopted."

The words came out so matter-of-factly

that Debbie was taken aback. "What?"

"I'm adopted. I always wanted to know who my real parents were. My mom told me some young thing gave me away when she was a teenager. I was a teenage birth. It always kind of got to me, though, thinking about being adopted, wondering if my real parents thought about me or how I turned out."

Debbie could hardly believe the words flowing out of Trish. It made her feel badly that she'd thought so little of her. She could have been more patient with Trish and more of a friend. Maybe it would have helped them both in the long run. "Wow, I'm sorry to hear that."

"Don't be. You have nothing to feel sorry for."

"I know how Neil felt when he heard his paternal grandparents weren't his blood relatives, that his father was adopted into the family. It was hard. I don't know the feeling myself."

"I just wish my stepdad wasn't so drunk all the time when I was growing up. Good thing my folks split when they did. And I know my adopted mom cared about me, until she died of breast cancer last year." Trish took hold of the cart and rolled it away. Debbie stared after her, dumbfounded over the confession. What was the proverbial saying — *Don't judge a book by its cover*? And here she had judged Trish big-time without asking God for wisdom and understanding.

Just then she heard a sound she didn't think she would ever hear again. Laughter coming out of Elvina's room. It jolted her like an electrical current passing through an outlet. Elvina and Harold were sharing stories of a bygone era and laughing away. It played like music to her ears. She couldn't help but shed a tear before a smile came forth to match the merriment. She couldn't wait to tell Neil. He needed a good laugh right now, almost as much as they did.

He stared, his brown eyes fixed. She could've waved her hand over them, and he wouldn't have blinked. "They laughed?"

"Yes, Neil. They laughed. Ho, ho, ho."

He swiped his hand through his hair. "And then you saw her take the pills Mrs. Whitaker gave her?"

"With a big glass of juice. And she looked different. Peaceful. Calm."

"Wow. I can't believe it. I was hoping of course. Praying up a storm that there might be a change. I'm glad, Debbie. Really glad." He took her hands in his. "How shall we

226

celebrate? Dinner out?"

"Actually I need your help. Dinner's at my place. Stir-fry."

He smiled. "Sounds good. After all this, I could eat up a storm. Hope you make enough."

She smiled a bit coyly. "Oh, there will be plenty."

Neil handed Debbie several peeled carrots and watched her slice them up. "That's an interesting tale, I must say. But it doesn't excuse past behavior, like how she treated both you and Gram."

Debbie dumped sliced carrots into a bowl. She had just finished telling Neil about Trish, expecting him to react the way she had upon hearing of Trish's past. He didn't. She sighed. Neil hadn't done anything she expected the past few weeks she had known him. She tried to keep her nerves in check, all the while wrestling with the idea of truly knowing the man standing beside her. "This isn't just a tale, Neil. It's a moving story. And it makes me understand Trish a bit better."

"There is no way one can understand a woman like that. I mean, I had a tough life growing up in a single-parent home. But I don't persecute insurance claimants just because I had no father."

"So what should I do? Treat her like an outcast for her many sins?"

Neil opened his mouth to spout out a retort, then clamped his lips shut. Finally he said, "You should do whatever God tells you."

"Good. Because I invited Trish to join us for dinner."

"You did what?" His gaze swept the counter. "No wonder you're cooking up enough to feed an army. And here I thought this was all for me."

"I hope that isn't a problem. Jesus ate with the outcasts, as I'm sure you know. And since you two have something in common, growing up in different family situations, I thought it would be good."

Just then she felt the sweep of his hand on hers. "Debbie, I don't care to eat with Trish."

"Huh?" The statement both startled and puzzled her.

"Hello?" He tapped her gently on the head. "We've had encounters in the past, none of which were overly pleasant. Before that, she and all the rest of her crew were like vultures after a kill. I don't care to give out any more mixed signals, especially since my signal is set."

"What do you mean, your signal is set? Set to what?"

He pried the knife carefully from her fingers and laid it on the counter. His touch sent a tremor through her. "I'll give you one guess." He drew near, pulling her into his embrace.

She wiggled out of his arms. "I know you may think your light is green, Nathaniel J., but mine is yellow and rapidly turning red." She grabbed a red Christmas hand towel and held it in front of her. "And if you don't watch it, the police will give you a little ol' ticket for running a red light." He withdrew, a grin still on his face, even as she picked up the knife again to tackle the veggies. "I wouldn't worry about Trish getting the wrong signal," she added. "She decided to also invite a friend. Her new boyfriend, I think. I told her you would be here and that you love computers. This guy does, too, it seems. So you two can chat."

His cheeks turned rosy. "Now you tell me. Thanks a lot, missy."

"You didn't ask." She felt like giggling the way his face contorted into a picture of discomfort. She continued to chop and dice, even as she sensed his gaze on her. The chemistry was so strong between them. She felt like a chemistry student, ready to watch her experiment in love boil over. Yes, this man was having a profound effect on her and growing by leaps and bounds as each day passed.

The feelings abruptly subsided when the doorbell rang. Neil went to answer it. Voices soon filled the living room. A sense of peace flowed through Debbie. God was good, even if things didn't look quite right in her eyes. He was in control.

Trish came to dinner bearing some new records for Neil's grandmother. "I thought maybe Elvina would like hearing some of these. They are left over from my stepmom. Guess I inherited them."

Debbie thought Neil would keel over right there. He gave a sheepish thank-you, avoiding eye contact. Debbie thanked God for the change she'd seen in Trish and for bringing her here.

"I see the guys are already talking about the latest computer games," Trish noted, moseying on into the tiny kitchen where Debbie was working. She helped herself to a carrot.

"Boys must have their toys. I took Neil shopping for his family the other day at the mall, and I could tell he only wanted to check out the computer store across the way from the bath boutique."

Trish laughed. "It's so typical, isn't it? Stu only wants to talk computers, too. I didn't even have a computer until he hooked me up. Now I love chatting with friends." She stood still, watching, even as Debbie sensed her own nervousness. "You know, I wonder why you and I never got along."

The comment took Debbie by surprise. "I'm not sure. I guess because we both do things differently."

"Well, you might as well know — I'm quitting White Pines after the New Year. I'm going to work in the same computer store as Stu, handling the cash register. I'm just not cut out to work at the facility anymore."

"You've been there a long time."

"Too long. It's time to move on. But I think you need to go on with nursing, Debbie. Go to college and get your degree. Become an RN like Mrs. Whitaker."

"Huh?" Debbie's knees turned to gelatin.

"Sure. You have what it takes. I mean, we all see it. Maybe that's why we've had problems. You're a natural at taking care of these people. Some of us, well, it's just a job. But to you, this is your life. You pour everything into these people's lives. You live for them really."

Debbie never imagined anyone observing her in such fine detail, except when she made a blunder. Now Neil's words of long ago came back — how her mission field was right where God had placed her, inside the White Pines Health Care Facility. She prayed she might make a difference. Come to find out, her life had been speaking loud and clear, more than mere words could say. "I do like it," she admitted. "I don't know, though, if I have the money and the stamina to become a full-fledged nurse. I see what Mrs. Whitaker has to do."

"My sister — actually my stepsister — is a nurse. She works in the ER and loves it. I wouldn't be caught dead handling gunshot wounds and all that. But you should really think about it."

"Maybe I will. Thanks." For the first time, Debbie could see going to the mall with Trish, or maybe a movie, as remarkable as that seemed a mere week ago. How rapidly things could change — and when she least expected it!

Dinner was a rousing success. While they ate dessert, Trish laid down her fork. "Hey, I want to make an announcement."

"You're engaged," Debbie said with a sigh. She tried to avoid Neil's eye as he turned to look at her.

"No way," Stu said loudly.

Trish laughed. "That will take some

convincing. Actually, Neil, I know that you were looking to hire a nurse to take care of Elvina over the holidays. Have you filled the post yet?"

"No," he answered, a bit cautiously.

"I told Trish she must have New Year's Eve off," Stu added. "I've got it set for us to go to Times Square to watch the ball drop."

"So since Neil needs a nurse for Christmas, do you want to switch with me, Debbie? I'll work Christmas if you'll work New Year's Eve. And that leaves you free to take care of Elvina if you want to."

Debbie could hardly believe it. And from the look on Neil's face, neither could he.

"I don't know what to say, Trish."

"Merry Christmas." She handed over her plate. "And another helping of that carrot cake, please. It's simply divine."

When the evening wrapped up and Trish and Stu said good night, Neil came to help Debbie with the dishes. She could only sing the praises of God for doing a great work. "Neil, I must admit, you were right again."

He nearly dropped the red dish towel. "I don't think I can handle all this praise, Debbie. It's giving me a swelled head. What did I do this time?"

"When you talked about our unique mission work, giving our jobs to God and letting Him use us . . . Trish said some really wild things tonight. Not only, of course, about switching holidays and all. But she commented on my work with the residents and thinks I should become an RN like Mrs. Whitaker. She says I have what it takes."

"I agree wholeheartedly. In fact, if you need a loan for school, I'd be happy to help out."

"What? But I haven't even decided if I'm going to be one or not."

"I think it's a great idea. And who would have thought your old nemesis would confirm it?"

No one. No one but God, that is. He had a knack for coming up with surprises in the most unexpected fashion. But becoming a nurse might mean jumping from the frying pan into the fire. Or it might mean the satisfaction of a dream fulfilled, to have a degree and a good job, like everyone else in her family. To feel a sense of accomplishment while doing something near and dear to her heart — caring for the injured, the aged, those in need. "Think I'll be any good at it?"

"Is that a trick question?"

"It might be. I'm asking you if you think this is something I should do, or is everyone just trying to be nice."

"I doubt Trish would say it just to be nice. She has nothing to lose or gain at this point. Maybe she's seen the light for the first time. I didn't tell you this, but when I was reading the Bible to Gram that day she refused to take her pills, I saw Trish standing outside in the hall. I wondered then if she had heard the words. Somehow I think this has really affected her."

Debbie couldn't help but agree.

"And as for me," Neil said, "I've been trying to be nice for a very long time and wondering if I'd been failing at it miserably. Especially when you wanted to leave this area and never return. It made me wonder if we were on the right track or not."

She didn't blame him for thinking that. He had been nice. In every word and deed, a true friend. And maybe more. Working side by side, doing dishes, and chatting, she felt completely at home with him. They seemed right for each other. She had seen the light, and maybe now her very own Christmas wish stood poised to become a reality.

Chapter 15

"This has been so wonderful; I don't know what to say."

Debbie watched from afar as Elvina sat with her grandchildren and great-grandchildren in Neil's mother's home, surrounded by gifts and love. The last two days had gone so well she could hardly believe it. Elvina was a different person — strong, determined, even able to take a few steps from her bed to the wheelchair. She acted younger. At times, she even seemed to see: She expounded on things that were happening all around her, such as when one of the great-nieces snitched a Christmas cookie from the plate. It had made a world of difference in her life to be here with her loved ones. And Debbie had to admit, it made a difference in hers, too, just to be here with Neil's family. At times, she caught members of his family looking at her strangely. Maybe he had mentioned their relationship to them in passing conversation. Or maybe they knew something she didn't.

She chuckled in hindsight, recalling the day Neil asked her to come and help during Christmas. Though she expected to hear about it after Trish's offer to exchange holidays, he hadn't mentioned anything until one day when he came knocking on her apartment door. He told her in an excited voice how everything was arranged. "We're set to have Gram come to my mom's house for Christmas. I tiptoed in with the issue to Mom, and she agreed, as long as I took care of all the details. I've arranged for the bed and the necessary supplies. I lack only one tiny detail."

"And what would that be, pray tell?"

He winked. "I need a certain nurse willing to help me out. The one who kissed me the other week at Christmastown, USA, would do nicely."

He opened his arms to pull her into his embrace, and they kissed again, right after she said, "I will." She half expected an engagement to follow on the heels of all this, but then again, Neil remained too absorbed with preparations for his grand-mother's Christmas visit for something that drastic. And rightly so. Though she did dream of the big night when he would whisk her away for a candlelight dinner and ask for her hand on bended knee. Maybe New Year's — the perfect time for a new beginning.

Debbie glanced at her watch. After the gift exchange, Neil left to run an errand. Why he felt the need to escape somewhere on Christmas morning, she couldn't imagine. No stores were open, as far as she knew. Ninety minutes had already passed. What could be keeping him?

She turned her attention to the Jenson family — Neil's mother giving Elvina a cup of juice; his sister, Sandy, talking to Elvina about her job; the two great-granddaughters looking over some new jewelry; and Neil's brother, Dick, immersing himself in the computer game Neil had given him. Both Neil's mother and Sandy loved their bath products in the baskets.

"Did you pick this out?" Neil's mother had asked him after unwrapping her gift.

Sandy laughed outright. "Oh, Mom, really. Can you imagine a guy buying bath products? Obviously he conned Debbie into doing it for him. You can see the woman's touch. You did it, didn't you, Debbie?"

Debbie remembered the loving glance Neil had given her, even as her fingers traveled over the pure black sweater he had wrapped up for her in bright Christmas paper. He laughed at the new black hat she had given him to match his black overcoat and black gloves. "Now I am definitely the man who wears black," he said with a chuckle.

"And it looks like you're getting Debbie to follow suit," Sandy added, pointing to the black sweater.

It didn't matter to Debbie. She loved the sweater, and yes, she had fallen in love with the man, too. They were made for each other, as he once said. Now she was getting edgy for his return. Without him here, she felt like an intruder among his family, even though she was hired to care for Elvina.

"Where could Neil be?" his mother asked.

"You know him," Sandy said. "He has something up his sleeve. Remember when he once came for Christmas with that puppy, Mom? I thought you would die when he said it was for you."

"Yes, and I gave the dog to a lonely member in my church who needed the companionship much more than I did. I only hope Neil gets back in time to help carve the roast. He's the only one who knows how to work my electric knife."

At last, Debbie heard the rumble of an engine and a car door slam.

"Debbie, can you give me a hand with this gift?" Neil called out. "It's very fragile."

Debbie offered a meek smile to the inquisitive looks displayed by the family before darting out the door. To her surprise, Harold sat in the front seat of Neil's car, grinning from ear to ear. "This is the best day of my life," he told them as they helped him into a portable wheelchair. "The best day. Look at that sun. Look at the blue sky."

"So this is your secret errand," Debbie murmured to Neil with a smile. "What will your family think?"

"He's just here for the afternoon. And besides, I'm not doing it for them. I'm doing it for Gram. This is her Christmas wish come true, in a way."

Debbie looked at him in confusion until it dawned on her — Elvina's wish that she learn what happened to her beloved Samuel. Harold was the link to it all. When they brought Harold into the house, Neil's family was on their feet in an instant.

"Why, Neil!" his mother exclaimed.

"What on earth are you doing?" Sandy added.

"I'm bringing Gram her special Christmas present, so don't say anything else," he announced, slowly wheeling Harold over to Elvina, who stared expectantly. "It's a present she specifically asked for." Then to his grandmother, he said, "Hold out your hand, Gram."

"Oh, dear. I hope you didn't get me anything too expensive or large, Nathaniel," she said. Neil took Harold's hand and placed it in his grandmother's. She grew rigid. "I — I don't understand." Her fingers traced the pathway of Harold's jagged veins and long, bony fingers.

"Merry Christmas, Liv."

Her hand fell away. "It can't be. Whatever are you doing here, Harold?"

He looked to Neil for help.

"Merry Christmas, Gram," Neil said with a laugh.

She turned white. "I don't understand. How is Harold my Christmas gift?"

Neil knelt beside her and took her other hand in his. "Gram, remember how you said you had one big Christmas wish, to know what happened to the man who means a great deal to you and to our family? The one who gave me a great dad, even if I never knew him? That's why Harold is here. He knew our real grandfather. He knew our dad. And he was the last one to speak to Sam before he left this world. He's the answer to your Christmas wish — in an indirect way, that is."

No one said anything for several agonizing moments. Debbie looked at each family member. Some wore expressions of disbelief. Neil's mother's eyes harbored tears. Debbie could barely draw a breath, wondering what would happen next. Would this special gift be accepted? Would the wounds from long ago find healing? Would the family open their hearts and accept Harold?

Finally Elvina turned to Neil. "Well, Nathaniel, are you going to put on a Christmas carol or two? I brought my record player and albums with me, you know."

Neil grinned. In no time, the bars of a favorite Christmas carol, "Joy to the World," filled the room. When they finished, the family pressed in around them, asking Harold about his friendship with their Sam and how he and Elvina had come to meet. Debbie never saw Harold so filled with warmth and love. What a far cry from just a few weeks ago, when he was but a sad and lonely man.

What a beautiful day, too. Now Debbie was witnessing a freedom in Harold's spirit, and in Elvina's, as well. They no longer held expressions of confusion, weariness, or dismay, but life and even love. When Harold's hand reached for Elvina's, taking it up in his own, Debbie's heart flip-flopped at the sight.

"I do have one other request to play," Neil announced. He took up another record, one of the older versions Debbie had purchased at the antique store a few weeks back. "This is Harold's gift to Gram." All at once, Harold's rich bass voice filled the room as he sang a love song from days gone by. Everyone chuckled in glee. Elvina sat there, mesmerized by the man who sang to her so lovingly.

Suddenly Harold brought forth a small box out of his shirt pocket. Before Elvina could say anything, he took out a ring and slipped it carefully on her ring finger. "Liv, will you marry me?"

"Harold . . . ," she began, her fingers touching the ring. "Oh, Harold!"

Debbie sucked in her breath in astonishment. Shock resounded throughout the family circle. Sandy sat unmoving, her eyes glued to the scene. Neil's mother stared with the same confused expression. "Don't you think you're moving a little fast with all this?" she wondered. "I mean, didn't you both just meet at White Pines a short time ago?"

Harold squirmed in his chair. Debbie sucked in her breath, wondering if she should say anything. She saw Neil slowly shake his head at her. This was Elvina and Harold's to handle. She could only watch and pray for God's will to come forth.

"I know it seems very fast," Harold began.

"Oh really, Terrie," Elvina remarked. "Look at us." A tear began sliding down her cheek. Her finger gently stroked the ring she held. She then lifted her face. A smile broke out. "I think two lonely people like us still have a few years left for happiness. Don't you?"

No one could say anything after that. When Debbie's gaze fell on Neil, he wasn't looking at the elderly gentleman proposing to his stately grandmother or responding to the questioning glances of his mother. He was staring straight at her.

While the family marveled at the Christmas Day engagement in their midst, Debbie went to fetch Elvina's medication for the afternoon. Her hand shook as she fumbled with the pills. She could hardly believe what had happened. One gift on top of the other. And she was here to see it all, thanks to Trish. *It's a fact. The Lord does work in mysterious ways.*

All at once, she heard footsteps behind her. She turned to find him leaning against the door frame, his arms folded. *Neil. Dear, sweet, thoughtful Neil.* She really did love him. What would be their future? More mysteries to solve? More places to explore? More hot chocolate to drink? Or maybe each other to have and to hold one day when the time was right?

"Great moment, huh?" he said.

"Wow, I should say. One for every history book and fairy tale there is. Weren't they cute? Who would have thought?"

"No one. At least not me — until Harold told me what he had in mind."

"So you knew Harold would propose?"

"He talked to me about it a few days ago. He said that Liv had done something miraculous in him. He couldn't stop thinking about her. He asked me what it was that made him feel that way. I said, 'Love, my man!' He wondered if they dared marry, if that could happen with their residence in White Pines. I said, 'Why not?' So he asked me to find an antique ring, something old but meaningful. We set this all up for today."

"Neil, you're something else. You really do like making wishes come true, don't you?"

"Only God can make it a reality. Sometimes what we wish for isn't always the best thing for us. But He can make it all come out right in the end. He is faithful."

She listened, deep in thought, wondering about her secret desire, if it was a part of

God's great plan or simply wishful thinking. But she knew better than to second-guess at this point. She had witnessed a wonderful miracle — and on Christmas morn, when the greatest miracle of all had come forth. On top of it all, she could delight in the love of a man God had brought into her life when she needed him most. "Yes," she agreed, allowing his arms to impart an embrace of warmth and of love. Their lips met. "He is very faithful, to the end."

EPILOGUE

The tiny White Pines chapel never looked more beautiful to Debbie. Red roses stood in a vase on the altar. Bows decorated the pews. And the time was perfect, too, for celebrating love, as Elvina and Harold exchanged their wedding vows that afternoon. *Valentine's Day. The day of love.* She exhaled a sigh, even as her gaze drifted over to Neil, standing beside Harold as his best man. How handsome he appeared in a dark suit and tie with a red-rose corsage pinned to the lapel. She steadied the bouquet of roses she held in her hands. The heavenly scent filled her. It was a blessed event come true, and one she hoped to experience in her own life. But for now she and Neil had made an agreement to take it slow. Take the time to know each other more. To seek God in everything. And allow their relationship to grow. Yet she couldn't help but think of her own wedding in the process. *I will definitely have roses,* she decided. *The red roses of love. And a dove white wedding dress with a long veil that reaches to the floor.*

When Harold and Elvina's wedding kiss came, followed by applause, tears filled Debbie's eyes. The newlyweds looked radiant as they moved up the aisle in their respective wheelchairs to the rear of the chapel where they would receive congratulations from family and friends. Debbie followed to take her place in the receiving line, when she felt the warmth of Neil's hand sliding into the crook of her elbow.

"You made it through the ceremony and didn't faint," he whispered. "See? I knew you would do fine."

Debbie smiled, recalling her nervous jitters just before the ceremony was about to commence. But peace ruled the day and her heart, and for this, she could only thank God. They came to stand with Elvina and Harold, greeting Elvina's children and grandchildren, along with a few staff members from White Pines. When Debbie caught sight of Trish and her intended, Stu, among the guests, she felt her legs tremble.

Trish showed Debbie her hand and the sparkling diamond. "It's official. See?"

"Congratulations. You both didn't waste much time."

Trish laughed. "Hey, we plan to open our own computer store in the next few months. So I told him if he wants me to be a partner, then he'd better make it official with a proposal. And I didn't mean a business contract either."

Debbie laughed along with Trish until a lump of emotion filled her throat. She cast a sideways glance at Neil. *What about us, God? What is Your will for us? Will I have a diamond ring, too, one day? I don't mean to be impatient. I guess I just need to be content, grateful for Neil and for what You have done in our lives.*

When the receiving line had come to an end and the gathering wandered toward the solarium for a small reception, Debbie stepped away for a breath of fresh air. She pushed back her damp hair and sighed, only to find Neil coming toward her.

"Well, you did it," she said, loosening his tie.

"Thanks, I was getting hot. So what did I do?"

"Made a wish come true. Or you were instrumental in bringing about a wish, I guess I should say. Maybe even more than a wish."

"Debbie, it took two. In more ways than one."

"I didn't do that much."

He raised an eyebrow. "Well, I could stand here and make a list of your many accomplishments, as well. But that would both make us pretty late for the reception and Gram a bit miffed. But before we go, I do want to let you in on a little secret."

"Yes?"

"I had a wish, too, like Gram. I could sing the Jiminy Cricket song of wishing on a star, but I can't sing worth anything. Besides, I took my wish to the One who knows what's best for me."

Debbie thought she might melt like a snowflake on the warm ground when she heard these words. If only she could tell him her desire, too — that she would love to spend a lifetime with him. *If only.* "So what might your wish be?"

When she saw the velvet box in his hand, she gasped. Their wishes were one and the same! "Me?"

"You. My one and only. Marry me?"

"Yes!" she cried with tears in her eyes. There was a special guy just for her in this whole wide world, and God knew it most of all.

Thank You, God. Wishes do come true.

ABOUT THE AUTHOR

Lauralee Bliss, a former nurse, is a prolific writer of inspirational fiction as well as a home educator. She resides with her family near Charlottesville, Virginia, in the foothills of the Blue Ridge Mountains — a place of inspiration for many of her contemporary and historical novels. Lauralee Bliss writes inspirational fiction to provide readers with entertaining stories, intertwined with Christian principles to assist them in their day-to-day walk with the Lord. Aside from writing, she enjoys gardening, cross-stitching, reading, roaming yard sales, and traveling. Lauralee invites you to visit her website at www.lauraleebliss.com.